FOR BETTER FOR BROKE

E M RICHMOND

Published by Leanne Warr (EMR Books)
Copyright ©2017 by E. M. Richmond
Cover: Copyright ©2017 by CarolsCoverDesigns.com

Also available as an e-book.

Dedication

For Carol and Meg

Disclaimer

The characters, settings and situations are entirely fictional. Any similarities to anyone living or dead is coincidental.

"When or if I ever get married, I want it to be for love. Not to solve my financial problems."

Kate Delaney finds life is a struggle. She is about to lose her job and has no idea how she is going to manage financially.

Her close friend Nick Sloane thinks he has the perfect solution. Marriage.

But Kate wants love, not what looks to be a marriage of convenience, no matter how she feels about Nick.

Chapter One

"Why don't we get married?"

Kate stared at Nick, her hand practically frozen in mid-air as she fought to swallow the tiny sip of wine she'd just taken. He reached out and touched her wrist, gently pushing it down so the bottom of her wineglass connected with the tabletop with only a slight clink.

She swallowed hard, her gaze flicking from the man opposite her to the wineglass.

"You were about to spill your drink," he responded mildly.

She frowned. "Huh?"

"Well, I know I kind of sprung it on you, Katie, but I didn't think you'd react quite like this."

Her frown deepened. "How - how did you expect me to react?" she asked. "You just said ... you just suggested ..."

"Getting married."

"Why?"

He looked taken aback at that, his dark eyebrows shooting up toward his brow. If Kate didn't know any better, she would have said he was actually hurt by the question. Nick was one of her best friends and a great guy, but he wasn't known for thinking things through. His mother would have called him impulsive.

"Well, I would have thought that was obvious," he said, his tone rather flat.

She shook her head. "Not to me." She brushed at some imaginary crumbs on the tabletop, her face burning hot.

"Well, it would solve all your problems. And a few of mine as well."

She hadn't been complaining as such. Kate tried never to complain about how bad her life was, figuring it was something her friend didn't need to hear. Nick was the one who had brought it up as soon as they'd sat down at the restaurant.

"What problems could you possibly have?" she asked, looking him over.

Nick Sloane was a good-looking man, although he would often say Kate was biased because they were friends. He had dark blond hair that tended toward unruly but often refused to use any kind of gel to tame it, preferring the 'wild man' look. Kate liked the way the short strands on each side of his head curled around his ears, while the hair from his crown flopped over his forehead, giving him almost a rakish devil-may-care look.

His eyes were an intense blue, almost topaz, with crinkles in the corners showing he laughed often and with great enthusiasm. That and his tendency to forget to wear the wire-rimmed spectacles he had been prescribed as a teenager. Not out of any kind of vanity but more out of an absent-mindedness.

He had a mole just on the blade of his left cheekbone, a tiny dark lump which he had told her had suddenly appeared when he was in his early teens and had remained ever since. Instead of detracting from his handsomeness, it just seemed to enhance it.

Usually clean-shaven, tonight Nick had a dark shadow of a beard. Kate knew it wasn't the fact that he didn't make an effort, even for her, but it was more that he had never really been the type of man to care about looks.

What could a man who looked like him possibly have to complain about, Kate thought.

"Problems? Katie, I've got problems like you wouldn't believe."

"Enlighten me, then."

He glanced over Kate's shoulder at something, or someone.

"There's a woman sitting behind you with a guy who looks old enough to be her father, but there's no way he could be because of the way they're acting. Anyway, she keeps looking over here and, well, you know that saying if looks could kill?"

Kate nodded. Of course she knew it. She wasn't surprised the woman was glaring daggers.

"The thing is, I get that all the time. Women are throwing themselves at me."

She wrinkled her nose. "How is that a problem?"

He huffed. "Aw come on. You studied this at uni, didn't you? All about the objectification of women? I mean, don't you see the double standard here?"

"It doesn't mean she's objectifying you," Kate pointed out. "I mean, last I heard, you didn't have the power to read minds, so you don't really know that's what she's thinking."

He snorted. "Please. Most of the women who throw themselves at me do it because they think I'm easy."

Kate sighed. "Okay, I'll give you that."

She knew for a fact that her friend hadn't slept with a woman in at least a year. As he often complained, the well had run dry. As if a year of celibacy was a major catastrophe, she thought cynically. Try five years. Or more.

"I'm still not sure I see what your problem is," she continued. "I mean, it can't be that much of a hardship to have women throwing themselves at you." She chewed on her lip. "It's not like I have guys throwing themselves at me." She tried not to sound bitter but it still came out that way.

"I'd rather they didn't," Nick replied. At least, that was what Kate thought she heard. He'd tilted his head down so she couldn't read his lips, a sure sign she wasn't meant to have heard him. Kate had been born partially deaf so it wasn't easy for her to understand people.

He looked up at her once more.

"Where was I?" he asked, smiling brightly.

"You were about to tell me your problems and how getting married would solve them."

"Well, think about it. Like I said, women practically throw themselves at me. Okay," he added, raising his hand as if she was about to raise an objection. "Maybe when I was younger that wouldn't have been such an issue. I admit it, okay? I liked it. I partied with the best of them. But that was then and this is now. Maybe I want to settle down with a nice girl. Have a family. I mean, I'm not getting any younger."

"You're only thirty-two."

"And my clock is ticking," he said.

She scoffed at him. "Men don't have a biological clock. Not like women do anyway. You'll still be capable of having kids when you're in your seventies. I mean, look at ... what was his name?"

"Who?" Nick asked with a frown.

"The guy that played Scotty on Star Trek. Didn't he have a kid when he was in his sixties or something?"

"Your nerd roots are showing," he retorted. She blew a raspberry at him.

"Are you ready to order?"

Kate frowned. She hadn't realised the waitress had approached the table. Nick smiled at the blonde, his gaze sweeping over her curvy body. The waitress was at least five years younger than Kate, who was thirty. Her blonde hair was cut in a cute pixie style that suited her round apple-shaped face.

Nick seemed to appreciate the waitress' looks as well, judging from the smile on his face. Kate kicked him under the table. The man had just suggested getting married and was looking at a waitress like she was the best thing since sliced bread.

He shot her a wounded look. "What?"

"Must you?" she asked.

The waitress looked confused. Kate picked up her menu and handed it to the girl with an apologetic look, rolling her eyes and indicating her companion. The woman smiled and winked at her in understanding.

"Could I have the Moroccan chicken salad please?" she asked politely.

The waitress nodded and wrote it down on her notepad with her left hand before turning back to Nick. Kate noted the ring on her finger and wondered if it was an engagement ring.

"I'd like the seafood platter," he said.

"Of course. Thank you."

"Seafood platter?" Kate asked as the woman walked away. "Rather a safe option, don't you think?"

"Unlike your Moroccan chicken," he shot back. "Think I want indigestion?"

She wrinkled her nose at him. The truth was, the only time she felt free to explore different cuisines was when Nick took her out for their weekly dinners. Most of the time she was forced to eat instant noodles or canned soup she had heated in the microwave.

Nick, of course, didn't know about her poor diet. Or if he did, he didn't bring it up. Her financial troubles had always been a sore spot in their friendship. Kate often refused to talk about it, since Nick usually took it as a sign she was asking for help. It was one thing Kate never would do.

Tonight the subject had reared its ugly head once again. Nick had somehow found out Kate was about to lose her job. Since he knew her boss fairly well, he had probably got the news from her. Joy had promised her niece she could work part-time in the gallery where Kate worked and that meant Kate had to find something else.

She didn't want to go back on the dole again but she didn't see that she had much of a choice. She still had debts to pay off and rent to pay. She'd only been working at the gallery a couple of years and while she didn't exactly get along with her boss, Joy at least acknowledged she was more than capable of doing the job.

Her boss had been clear from the start the role had only been temporary as she was waiting for her niece to finish school. Despite that, the money Kate had earned still wasn't enough to ease the financial pressure.

Of course, she had been stupid enough to fall for a guy who had basically been a drop-kick. He had borrowed money from a finance company to buy an expensive car, then borrowed more money from another finance company to modify the car so he could race it with his mates. Unbeknownst to Kate, he'd made it a joint loan and forged her signature on the documents. When he'd died after crashing the car in a race, the car hadn't been insured and he had no life insurance. He'd left Kate with a debt of thousands of dollars still owing.

She had thought about declaring bankruptcy, but it was the last thing she wanted to do after watching her parents go through it.

Lately, however, the creditors had been applying more pressure and demanding more and more money. Kate knew they were loan sharks and she could have fought back by taking them to court, but she couldn't face that kind of humiliation. She didn't want people judging her for what she felt was her own stupidity for even trusting the man in the first place.

It had been going on for five years and there was still no end in sight.

The clink of glass against glass as her wine glass was refilled brought her back to the present.

"Welcome back," Nick said. "Where were you?"

"Someplace scary," she replied, shooting him a look which told him not to push for further information.

He grinned and shrugged, unfazed. "Yeah. I hear that. So, where were we?"

"You were talking about your biological clock, which, as I pointed out, is a complete misnomer."

"Yeah, tell that to my mother," he said gloomily.

"What about your mother?"

"She's not getting any younger, you know."

Kate looked at her friend. "So you're saying … what? She wants grandchildren?"

"Well, yeah."

Nick was an only child. His father had left his mother about two years after Nick was born. While he never talked about it, Kate wondered if there had been some domestic abuse. She was no psychologist, but she did get that impression from the little he did say about it. He had told her he had visited his father only a half-dozen times in his childhood and had had little to do with him ever since.

The waitress returned with their meals. Kate dug into her chicken dish with gusto, loving the combination of spices. Nick's seafood platter looked just as appetising.

They dined fairly regularly at the restaurant. It helped, Kate supposed, that the restaurant was close to Nick's office and he often entertained corporate clients there. It was small and intimate, yet also clean and modern in décor. Kate had always liked the fact that the restaurant would close for a week around the same time every year in its lowest season for refurbishing, re-opening with a fresh look. She had been in some restaurants that hadn't been updated for years and it showed from the dilapidated furnishings and poor lighting to the cracks in the leather upholstery.

The Blackwater Bistro was family-owned and the owners clearly cared about their clientele. For regulars like Kate and Nick, they were treated practically like family.

Wanting to distract Nick from his 'proposal', Kate picked up some of the spiced chicken on her fork and held it to him. He frowned at her.

"Hell no," he said.

"Come on. Live a little."

He cocked an eyebrow at her. "Miss Hospital Corners is telling me to live a little?"

"I am not Miss Hospital Corners," she retorted. "I am not that high maintenance."

In the early days of their friendship, Nick had invited her to watch a few movies with him and his friends. One of those friends had brought an old romantic comedy in which the lead female character had been high maintenance. The leading man had called her 'Miss Hospital Corners'. When Nick had got to know her better and learnt she liked things a certain way, he'd teased her with the same line.

"Really? Oh, I beg to differ."

"Okay, name one time."

"Last week."

She frowned at him. "What about last week?"

"You freaked out because I parked in a loading zone. Outside of business hours!"

"Loading zones are supposed to be kept clear at all times," she told him, bristling at his mild rebuke. Rules were rules, she thought. He shrugged his shoulders in a gesture that suggested he was indifferent to it. She knew she could be fairly rigid about some things but he could either like it or lump it.

"Like I said, Miss Hospital Corners."

She scowled at him. "You suck!"

He snorted. "Fine. I suck. You're still not gonna get me trying that stuff."

"Wuss!"

He sniggered. "Yeah, I'm the wuss. You won't even answer my question."

"What question is that?" she said with a sigh, although she had a fair idea.

"About getting married."

She made a sound like a buzzer from a game show, like a contestant who had chimed in with the wrong answer.

"No, but thanks for playing!'

"Come on, why not? Like I said. It would solve your problems. I mean I could help you with your finances."

"So you're suggesting something like a marriage of convenience?"

"Well, yeah. I mean, I guess."

She stared at him, feeling an irrational surge of anger. Part of her knew what he was trying to do but it still irked that he thought money would just make all her problems disappear.

"Do I look like a charity case to you?"

He looked at her, his fork halfway to his mouth, then lowered his hand carefully, taken aback by her comment. It had come out a little angrier than she had meant it to. She wanted to apologise but the harsh words were already out there.

She had never liked being poor. It had always felt like other people looked down on her because of it, even though the rational side of her told her that most people probably didn't even know her and wouldn't have been thinking anything of the sort.

Nick had certainly never cared. They might have been raised differently but he often told her he judged people by their actions, not by their looks. As far as he was concerned, being rich or poor didn't guarantee happiness.

It still hurt though, she thought.

"Uh, that's not what I meant," he said slowly.

"Then what did you mean?"

"I, well, I just thought, you know, that it would help. I mean, I'm just trying to ..."

Again, she felt that annoyance that he thought something like this could be fixed instantly, like there was some kind of magic button he could press which could change everything. He knew better than that.

"That's your problem, Nick. Half the time you just don't think!"

Her appetite gone, she pushed her plate away and took her napkin from her lap, throwing it down on the table. She couldn't even look at him.

She couldn't face the awkward silence that followed. Nick returned to eating his dinner, but Kate just couldn't. She sat fidgeting, bumping her knee against the underside of the tabletop, but it didn't help.

Unable to deal with the sudden brick wall between them, Kate got up.

"Where are you going?" Nick said, frowning at her.

"I'm suddenly not very hungry."

He stood up, reaching out a hand to her as if to stop her. "Stay," he insisted.

She shook her head. "No. Sorry, but I'm just not up to the company."

She walked out of the restaurant, conscious of the stares from the other diners. Nick was still standing at the table, staring after her in confusion. She had half-expected him to chase her but even if he had she would have turned him away.

She practically ran all the way home to her bedsit, despite it being at least a couple of kilometres from the restaurant. It wasn't until she closed the door behind her that the tears began to fall.

It was stupid and irrational, she thought, but she couldn't help it. Nick could never have realised when he suggested it that it would hurt her this much. How could he possibly have known how she really felt about him?

Chapter Two

Kate scowled at her reflection in the mirror. No matter how much make-up she used, she just couldn't seem to get rid of the bags under her eyes.

She had tossed and turned most of the night thinking over what had happened the night before. Nick had sent her a text message asking if she was okay, but she hadn't had enough credit on her phone to be able to text him back.

God, she was such an idiot, she thought. She realised Nick was just trying to help, even if the idea of them getting married was something totally out of left field. For a moment though, she'd actually entertained the notion, hoping something good might come out of it. Of course then she'd had to go and ask that stupid marriage of convenience thing.

It was so easy for him, she thought. Nick had it all. Charm, good looks, brains. He hadn't wanted for much growing up, since his mother had come from a fairly wealthy family. Then there was his six-zero salary. She couldn't begrudge him that, since he had worked damned hard to get where he was. His job wasn't exactly the kind where he could just put his feet up on the desk and watch his minions at work. Sure, he delegated some tasks but as CEO he took his role of company leader very seriously.

It was no picnic being the boss of a major publishing company, especially one that was constantly having to change to keep up with the latest trends. Or so Nick would complain.

Kate sighed heavily as she picked up her makeup compact and applied some of the pressed powder to her pale face. She supposed she was pretty enough. Her looks reminded her of a doll she had once had: skin as smooth as that doll's, with slightly chubby cheeks and a light blush. Lips just the right side of plump with a perfect bow, the dark pink shade needing little colour to enhance them.

Nick would often say she had the perfect look for a girl of her genetic make-up. Still, her flaming red hair and freckles made her feel like she wouldn't be out of place in the fictional Weasley household.

She remembered Nick making a comment on her curly red hair, saying it went with her temperament. Okay, she thought, so she had the Irish temper. Her great-grandfather, bless him, had been known for his sudden outbursts and his fiery Irish temperament, but the man would have given the shirt off his back to someone in need.

He'd left Northern Ireland amidst an atmosphere of hatred. The then teenage Frederick Delaney had been afraid for himself, wanting to get away from the mounting tensions between the Protestants and the Catholics. He had swapped the bitter hostility and the back streets of Belfast for the streets of urban New Zealand, taking a job as a storeman in one of the city's department stores.

It had been not long after that that the Great Depression had hit worldwide and like many others, Frederick lost his job when the department store had to close down some of its business. He had taken odd jobs, mostly labouring, where he'd met the woman who would become his wife. They'd both decided to travel further south and try for jobs in the smaller towns and had ended up settling in a small farming community.

The one thing Frederick had passed down through the generations was that nothing was ever for free. That no one ever achieved anything without hard work. Kate often wondered if her great-grandfather was right about that. He'd worked hard all his life but at the end of it, when he'd passed away at the age of eighty-four, there hadn't been much left. What little there had been to inherit had been shared between four siblings, some of whom had chosen to squander it.

None of them had ever really learnt to save money and it was a lesson that seemed to be passed down through the generations. They were a poor family and bitter with it.

Kate's father had often complained there was no money left over at the end of the week but he'd failed to take into account the fact that all the money he had earned had gone to pay debt, like credit cards and hire purchases. Her parents had wanted the luxuries but weren't prepared to wait for them, instead of paying exorbitant fees and interest.

Kate had learnt the hard way and had reasoned that if there was something she wanted, she could wait until she saved the money for it. Until she'd met Luke. He'd wanted the instant gratification instead of waiting for it, just like her father. Now because of him, she was facing bankruptcy.

She sighed. It was no good going around and around in circles and blaming the past. The only thing she could do was keep chipping away at it a little at a time. There was no way she was going to ask Nick for help.

It wasn't that she didn't appreciate the gesture. They were friends after all, and friends helped each other out. Still, getting married to a man she considered her best friend, her only friend, wasn't going to change her feelings about it. Especially because it wasn't going to be a real marriage, except on paper.

Her phone beeped a reminder that she only had a few more minutes before she had to leave for work. She checked her reflection again.

Ugh, she thought. She'd used too much powder and now her skin looked orange. She grabbed a wet wipe and did her best to fix the problem. She had let herself get distracted once again by Nick's proposal.

She didn't know why she bothered with the make-up sometimes. Joy certainly didn't seem to care either way. Langston Gallery was a little out of the way and only those who had a real interest in local artists tended to visit more frequently, so she didn't have as much contact with customers as she had thought she would when she took the job.

It was a job, though not for much longer, she lamented silently.

She grabbed a pair of black trousers from the rail, huffing in annoyance at the mark on one leg. She ran a cloth under the tap and rubbed at the mark, to no avail. Sighing, she put the trousers on and used a safety pin to lock the zip in place. The pants had been cheap because the zipper had been broken and she hadn't been able to fix it. Kate slipped a top over her head. It was an apricot colour which didn't really suit her complexion but she was just about out of time.

She frowned critically at her reflection. The clothes were baggy. They had fit reasonably well when she had bought them at the thrift shop a few months earlier but she'd lost a bit of weight since then.

Finally she slipped her feet into sneakers. She had run out of money on her bus card so would have to walk to work. It was a good thing it was reasonably cool as she hated being overheated when she finally did reach her destination. The gallery was situated in an old heritage building and budget constraints prevented the building's owners from installing air conditioning.

She had no idea what she was going to do once the job was over. Part of her resented Joy for basically kicking her out the door in favour of family but another part was resigned to it. She didn't want to get into a fight with her boss about it. Nick, she was sure, had already tried to talk to the older woman. He had just about come to blows with her once when Joy had threatened to fire Kate over something she hadn't even done.

She locked up the little flat and began walking, hands in her pockets and eyes downcast. She wasn't in the mood to offer a smile to any passers-by and was oblivious to the looks she received. A former friend had once told her she seemed aloof to others in the street and often people she knew would tell her they had called out to her or waved to her but she had ignored them.

Most didn't know that she usually became lost in her own world when she walked. She didn't listen to music since she could only half hear it anyway but her mind would drift.

So she didn't even hear or see the car pulling up beside her, or Nick getting out of the car and chasing after her.

Kate was startled by the hand on her arm. She turned, ready to defend herself against attack. Her eyes widened when she saw her friend. Nick had raised his hands in a gesture of surrender.

"Don't shoot," he said.

She shoved him with one hand. "Very funny."

"Can I offer you a ride to work?" he asked.

"Don't you have a staff meeting to get to?" she replied, knowing full well he held weekly meetings with his staff early on Friday mornings - the upside being that they could leave an hour earlier or stay and share a few drinks.

"Way to answer a question," he returned. She rolled her eyes at him. "Aw, come on, Katie. Lighten up!"

She scowled at him. "Was there something you wanted?" she said crossly.

"Look, I know you got a little upset last night. I get it, okay? I went about it all wrong. Just ..."

She kept walking. Nick moved quickly to catch up with her.

"Katie, come on. Talk to me."

"There's nothing to talk about," she said.

He began walking backwards, facing her.

"Katie ..."

She stopped walking and looked at him.

"Fine. You want an answer? My answer is no, Nick. Now go away and leave me alone!"

He shook his head. "I can't do that. Katie, you're in trouble. I just want to help."

She huffed. "By marrying me? How does that solve anything? I mean, sure, you say it would solve all your problems and please your mother, but what is she going to think when you tell her you're marrying a woman who has nothing to bring to the marriage. Look at me, Nick. I'm wearing clothes from the Op Shop, for crying out loud! I can't even afford to put food on the table and I'm living in a craphole! You know what people say about a person who marries for money?"

He shook his head in denial.

"The last thing you are is a gold-digger, Katie."

"They won't think so."

"They don't know you."

She waved her hands impatiently and started to move past him.

"We have nothing in common," she said. "We're from completely different worlds!"

"Opposites attract all the time," Nick argued.

"This has nothing to do with opposites attracting. This is you offering a marriage of convenience!"

"I'm not the one who said it," he reminded her.

"But you said, and I quote: 'Yeah. I guess.'"

"That's not a quote. When you're quoting someone, you usually quote them verbatim."

"Semantics!" she hissed.

They were drawing stares from other people in the street. Kate flushed, feeling suddenly very uncomfortable by the attention they were attracting.

"Nick, just, please go away. I don't want to have an argument with you in the middle of the street!"

"So you're not even going to let me plead my case?" he asked.

"You don't even have a case!" she replied, walking away from him.

"Why won't you let me help you, Katie?" he asked plaintively.

"Because!"

"That's not an answer!"

She turned and looked at him. "It's the only answer you're going to get."

He made a sound almost like a growl, deep in his throat.

"You know something Delaney, you are the most stubborn, most irritating woman I've ever had the misfortune to know. And I've known some!"

"Well, that explains why we're friends then," she replied. "Because the feeling's mutual."

He looked at incredulously. "I am not stubborn!"

"No? Then why are you still arguing with me?"

He stared back at her. "Uh, well …"

"I rest my case," she returned. "Go to work Nick."

"At least let me drive you," he said.

"No thanks. You drive like Brockie on a bad day."

Nick wasn't a bad driver, per se but he tended to be a little heavy-footed on the accelerator. His idol growing up had been Australian race car driver Peter Brock. He'd once told Kate he had wanted to follow his idol in the field but his mother had refused to contribute anything, saying he had to talk to his father. Nick had told her he'd gone to see his father, one of the few times he'd had anything to do with the man, but Gavin had barely even acknowledged his son, let alone provided the funds to finance Nick's first car.

"Do not!" he returned.

"Do too. Goodbye Nick." She stalked off, leaving him standing in the middle of the street.

Chapter Three

Kate made it to work just on time. Joy frowned at her as she entered the gallery and sat down at her desk. The older woman was rather fastidious in nature and had often criticised Kate for her timekeeping, despite the fact that nine times out of ten she would be at work at least fifteen minutes early.

"Cutting it rather fine, aren't you?" her boss asked, approaching the desk.

She wasn't going to tell Joy why she had been held up. The one thing that had been made very clear from the first day was that the older woman had no patience for personal problems. As far as she was concerned Kate's real life didn't exist once she was at her desk.

It made things difficult when Nick often popped in for a coffee or to share her lunch break with her. Kate got the impression that Joy would have booted him out the door if he hadn't been on the gallery's board, or his best friend hadn't been an artist. The gallery, she had told Kate pompously after Nick had dropped in one afternoon, was a place of business and not a place for socialising.

It was kind of ironic since that was how she and Nick had met two years earlier.

Joy had asked her to host an exhibition opening one evening. Kate had only just started at her job as an administrator a month earlier and she had no idea how to run such an event. Fortunately, her boss had provided her with a speech and the only thing she had to do was mingle among the guests and ensure they were sufficiently entertained.

Kate had had nothing to wear and since the exhibition was due to start half an hour after her working day ended, she had no time to go out and buy something. Joy had been a little friendlier in those days and she had offered Kate a dress that no longer fit her. The older woman, who was in her late thirties, had been fairly large at the time; while Kate had not quite been slim, she wasn't hugely overweight either.

The dress in question had been an ugly grey wool dress that itched when Kate put it on. It was almost a slate grey, which didn't go well with Kate's red hair and pale skin. Her complexion had been more suited to warmer colours. Her mother had often told her that the warm reds and browns she favoured put colour in her cheeks.

Nevertheless, she wore it to please her boss, who had smiled as she left the gallery.

Kate made sure all the food which had been brought in by the caterers was well-presented. She had never been much for rich food and finger sandwiches and asparagus rolls were as fancy as she could tolerate. She raised her eyebrows at the expensive caviar and salmon appetisers along with the cheese board consisting of gourmet cheeses like Stilton, Blue Cheese, Feta and Gouda. At least there was a vegie platter, she thought while eyeing the carrot and celery sticks.

She opened the doors right on five-thirty and dutifully welcomed the first guest. For the next fifteen or twenty minutes they slowly trickled in. Kate made sure they could help themselves to the wine or juice available and greeted the reporter from the local newspaper who had come to cover the exhibition.

She was talking to one lady in her late sixties, when Nick walked in. She was not the only one who noticed his presence. Nick walked like he owned the room. Good-looking seemed an inadequate description. Hot was close enough, even though she disliked the term. Kate stared at him for a few moments, then realised how rude that was before turning back to the elderly lady.

She did her best to greet all the newcomers and it was a while before she could get to Nick, who had been grabbed by the nearest guest and engaged in conversation. He smiled at her when she finally approached him.

"Hello," he said. "I'm Nick Sloane. I take it the guest-of-honour still hasn't arrived yet?"

Kate frowned at him. She hadn't met the artist, since all the details of the exhibition had been handled by Joy, so she wouldn't have known him if he'd walked in unless he'd introduced himself. She did recognise Nick's name because he was on the board of trustees. His mother, Diane, was also on the board and claimed to not have an artistic bone in her body. There was a distant relative who did, but had never been well-known. She had chosen to support the gallery to give other artists the opportunity that had never been afforded her relative.

Nick chuckled. "Don't worry. He'll be here, if he can pry himself away from the latest love of his life." He rolled his eyes in a put-upon expression, forcing Kate to laugh in response.

"You're a friend of his?" she asked.

"Yeah. Perry and I grew up together."

He eyed her with a curious look and she realised she hadn't even introduced herself.

"Oh. Um, I'm Kate Delaney. Joy asked me to host this evening."

He grinned. "Let me guess. She had a 'family emergency'. Joy's an old, uh, friend, friend being a relative term, of my mother's but she has a habit of ducking out on these things." He looked her up and down appreciatively. "Well, I must say, you're prettier than the last lady she hired to work for her."

Kate looked at him, a little taken aback. "Um, thank you."

Another guest came in the door and Nick turned. "About time, mate," he said, holding out his hand. The other man shook it, his blue eyes twinkling.

"Sorry. Got caught up. You know how it is." Perry turned to her and looked at her in a similar way to Nick, but his expression made her feel more than a little uncomfortable. Kate was annoyed by the other man's look. He was a good-looking man with dark brown hair and laughing brown eyes but she found his gaze a little disconcerting. "Well, hello. You're not Joy."

"No, she's not," Nick told his friend, nudging him in the ribs and receiving a sharp look for his trouble. "Be nice."

"Well, she's prettier than the last one. Have you warned her to watch her back? You know what Joy's like."

Kate frowned at the man, wondering what he meant by that. A glance at the clock told her it was time to get things started so she grabbed the speech Joy had written and called for everyone's attention.

Despite the words in front of her, she had no idea if what she had said emerged as English or gibberish. All she was aware of was the extremely attractive man watching her from the back of the crowd, sending a smile of encouragement as her nerves got the best of her and she faltered.

By the time the opening night was over, she was exhausted. She was supposed to clean up after all the guests had gone but it was already late and she couldn't face the thought of having to do all of that and then walk home. The last bus had already gone for the night.

To her surprise, Nick stayed behind and began picking up the trays.

"You don't have to do that," she told him.

He shook his head. "You're dead on your feet," he told her, waving away any effort to stop him. She didn't have the energy to argue.

The cleaning took little time at all and Nick walked her out the door.

"Where are you parked?" he asked.

"Oh, um, I don't have a car," she said. "I was just going to …"

"You can't walk home at this time of night," he told her. "It's Friday night. All the students will be out on their usual pub crawls."

Kate nodded, seeing his point. The city was notorious for its student population who tended to congregate in the centre of town, hitting all the bars and causing drunken fights. As the winter term approached, a good percentage of them did calm down and become more focused on their studies but a few still spent more time partying than studying.

"Let me drive you home," Nick said.

Kate bit her lip. She lived in a tiny studio flat at the back of an old house that had been converted into flats. Nick seemed like a nice guy - someone she would like to get to know. The last thing she wanted was for him to see just what kind of place she lived in. The house was at least one hundred years old and in extremely bad shape. The landlord was more interested in getting rent money than in keeping the house up to code.

Nick clearly wasn't going to take no for an answer, even going so far as to wait until she had opened the door and switched on the light before driving off.

A few days later, he showed up to take her out to lunch. Then it was dinner one night. Again he dropped her off practically at her doorstep.

Their friendship developed over several months but Kate didn't tell Nick about her financial problems. He would eventually find out, however, after she received what amounted to a threatening phone call at work. It was from the finance company owner telling her that if she didn't start paying more money he was going to send a collection agent around to take everything she owned. Since Kate had rented the flat furnished, there was nothing for the agent to take, but the man didn't seem to care.

Nick, overhearing the phone call and seeing her upset, managed to get the whole story out of her. While he didn't say anything, she knew he was worried. They'd known each other close to a year and a half by that time and she had managed to avoid his questions about her lifestyle. As much as she liked him, she didn't want to burden him with her problems.

Joy, on the other hand, was totally unsympathetic. Kate had never told her the whole story, but her boss had somehow managed to find out. She was dismissive, telling Kate to 'suck it up'.

Kate tried not to think bad of people, but Joy wasn't the easiest person to get along with. She had heard that the older woman had been widowed very early in her first marriage and her husband had been the love of her life. She had been married twice more since then but both of those marriages had ended in divorce. Joy was the complete opposite of her name. Bitter and angry at the world, she took it out on everyone. Kate often bore the brunt of her boss' moods.

Kate tried not to be negative and most of the time she was just dealing with it all in the best way she knew how. Still, that didn't mean she was going to treat her problems lightly. Nick wasn't too shy to tell her when he thought she needed to buck up. Still, it was so easy for him, she thought. He'd been born with the proverbial silver spoon in his mouth.

That wasn't to say he didn't have problems - his absent father being one of them. He refused to let that get to him. He often told her it wasn't the situation that was important, but the manner in how he dealt with it.

Kate remembered a weekend when their friendship had first begun. She'd had no idea where the relationship was going but she liked spending time with him. Nick could make her laugh and help her forget her troubles for a while.

That weekend, he'd called her and invited her to join him with Perry and a few of his friends. Nick picked her up outside her house but didn't tell her they would be driving to another city at least two hours away. On the way, Nick stopped to pick up Perry and his friend's latest 'love of his life'.

It was a beautiful summer's day and Nick drove with the windows down and the car stereo blasting music from an era just before Kate was born. Perry began singing along, rather badly. When he tired of that, he told terrible jokes which only seemed to get more bawdy as he went on.

Kate had never laughed so much in her life. She remembered turning to Nick and rolling her eyes in exasperation before laughing at his expression.

The trip wasn't over when they got to the city. Nick told her one of his friends owned a boat - a modestly-sized catamaran. They spent the day cruising the harbour, which was surprisingly calm for an area notorious for gale-force winds.

By the time Nick drove her home, Kate was a little tired, but pleasantly so. Nick smiled at her.

"You look like you could fall asleep right there," he said.

"Mm," she replied. "I had a nice day. Thank you."

"You seem surprised. I am capable of showing a girl a good time, you know."

She bit her lip. "I know, it's just … I don't know. I'd almost forgotten what it's like to just do something fun for the sake of having fun."

"Yeah, I figured that," he replied quietly. "Don't get me wrong, Katie. You're a great girl, but sometimes you take life too seriously."

She wanted to argue the point, but he was right. She listened as he continued on.

"My job can be stressful, but I learnt a long time ago to keep that stress where it belongs. At work. I work hard but I play hard too." He looked at her, putting a hand on her knee in a comforting gesture. "All that worrying, it's not good for you."

Blinking away the sudden tears that threatened as she pushed away the memory, Kate took a few deep cleansing breaths and settled down to work on a new brochure for the gallery. She couldn't help thinking about Nick's proposal. He made it sound so simple but she was used to having to jump over hurdles. It couldn't really be as simple as he suggested.

She pretended to focus on her work but couldn't help thinking over the past two years. Falling in love with the man she had come to think of as her best friend had been gradual. She knew some people believed in love at first sight but Kate had never really thought it existed. The one thing she did believe in, however, was that a lasting love needed a solid foundation. They were friends, but there had never seemed any possibility of anything more.

That was what made Nick's proposal so difficult. If she'd been any other girl who looked at the world with rose-coloured glasses, she probably would have jumped at the chance to be married to her best friend. If he'd given her any indication that there was a mutual attraction, Kate would have said yes in a heartbeat.

"Are you listening to me?"

Kate looked up and realised she had drifted off while Joy had been trying to get her attention.

"Sorry," she said apologetically. "I was miles away."

"Well, it's a good thing my niece is coming in next month."

She stared at her boss, wondering if that meant what she thought it meant.

"So, next Friday will be your last day, okay?"

A week? She had one week to get another job. Well, that was just great!

Chapter Four

The next week was a nightmare. Now that Joy had told her the date of her last day it seemed like the older woman considered she now had licence to treat Kate however she pleased. She was highly critical, complaining that the work was sub-par and not up to the standard she expected.

Joy became even worse on Kate's last day at the gallery. She gazed with disdain at her employee's choice of outfit. Kate had gone for a simple black skirt with a blouse in forest green. The colour suited her complexion and went well with her red hair. That clearly wasn't good enough for the older woman who looked at her over the rims of her reading glasses.

"A little unprofessional, don't you think?"

Kate frowned at her. Joy was hardly one to talk, since she was wearing jeans so tight she almost had camel-toe. She looked down at the skirt, which came to just above her knees standing up. She'd worn black pantyhose and high-heeled shoes in the same colour.

"Just a word of advice. From me to you. You shouldn't wear a skirt that short. Your legs are a little chunky. You're never going to find yourself a man if you wear outfits like that. You might think men like women to have it all out on show but that just makes you look cheap. Trust me, no one respects a woman who dresses like a whore."

Kate stared at her, taken aback by the woman's bitchy comments. She didn't think her outfit was that bad. In fact, it was fairly modest. She had lost quite a bit of weight in the past two years and the blouse was a little loose-fitting.

If she had been a different kind of person, Kate would have told her boss a few home truths. She opted to keep her thoughts about the other woman to herself and tried not to let it get to her. The situation was bad enough without her resorting to some kind of petty revenge. She was already well aware there would be no good reference from her boss, but responding to the woman's hateful remarks would make a bad situation even worse.

She had spent much of the past week looking for a new job; even contacting local recruitment agencies to see if they had anything on offer. So far none of them had bothered to reply to her tentative enquiries. The job market was a little slow, which was unusual for the time of year.

Nick had called a couple of times the previous weekend but she had missed the calls both times and still had no credit on her phone to be able to pick up any messages. Most evenings she had been spending at the library, since she didn't have a computer at home.

Joy had demanded Kate finish the brochure she was working on before she could leave, although it was unlikely the woman would pay her any overtime. Kate set to work with a heavy sigh, wishing she could just get up and walk out. Her work was not likely to be done to the older woman's satisfaction by closing time.

Her boss went out late morning, obviously expecting Kate to greet any visitors to the gallery. It was a warm, sunny day and it was not unusual for them to have a quiet day. Kate continued to work quietly, not expecting Joy to be back any time soon. So she was surprised to hear the older woman's throaty laugh in the foyer shortly after two.

She looked up and frowned. Joy was chatting with a tall man, whose back was to her. The other woman kept touching his arm, relentlessly flirting with him. Kate tried to ignore it but her soon to be ex-boss' double standard infuriated her. For someone who continually reminded Kate that the gallery was not a place for socialising she was breaking every rule in her book. Kate pretended to be focused on her work but could see in the corner of her eye the way the woman tossed her bleached-blonde head back and smiled in blatant invitation.

What galled was when the man turned around to enter the office. It was Nick. He frowned at her.

"Still working?" he asked.

"Oh, Kate's a real trooper," Joy told him cheerfully. "I told her since it was her last day she could leave early, but she volunteered to stay so she could finish the brochure she's been working on."

Oh, you lying … Kate turned back to her computer screen before she could spit out the insult she really wanted to give her boss. Joy shot her a glare but then turned the full force of her toothy smile at Nick. He frowned down at the other woman.

"Wait? Did you say it was Kate's last day? When did this happen?"

"Didn't Kate tell you?" Joy laughed. "I bet she forgot, the silly girl. She'd forget her head if it wasn't screwed on."

Kate didn't like the way Nick was practically glowering at her, as if she hadn't told him on purpose. She saved her work and started to gather her things, refusing to put up with the woman's two-faced behaviour anymore.

"Well, I'm done," she said. "I saved the brochure so you can have a look at it later." Meaning the other woman would be stuck doing edits, but Kate was beyond caring.

"I'm sure it will be fine," Joy said. "You've done a great job. I'm <u>so</u> sorry to see you go, Kate. You know if there was the budget I would have kept you on, but I did promise my niece ..."

Kate could see a little tic in Nick's jaw. He was angry about something but she wasn't sure exactly what it was.

"How about I give you a ride home, Katie," her friend suggested quietly.

Joy sent him a smile. "You are so good to help her out, Nicky." She faked a sympathetic sigh. "Poor Kate. I worry about her having to walk home all that way."

Her words would have sounded sincere if it wasn't for the condescension in her tone. Kate walked out without looking back, knowing if she had to listen to the vile woman's comments anymore she was liable to strangle her.

Nick followed her out a moment later, grabbing her arm.

"That evil, condescending ... I swear I was about ready to throttle her." He looked at her with a sympathetic smile. "Are you okay?" he asked. "Why didn't you call me?"

She shook her head. "I didn't have any credit on my phone."

"You could have just called the company. They would have put you through."

"Nick, don't. Please? I'm really not in the mood."

He relented, gazing down at her. "I bet you haven't had any lunch either." He gently guided her toward his car. "Come on. Let's get some food into you."

She sighed and shook her head. "Nick ..." The mention of food reminded her that she hadn't seen him in a week, which meant they hadn't had their usual dinner at a local restaurant. Her stomach rumbled noisily.

"No good protesting, Katie. I can hear your stomach growling."

She rolled her eyes but got into his car. He grinned at her before starting the car and driving off, ignoring the beep from an irate driver behind him.

"Sorry we missed our usual dinner date last night," he said. "I've been down south, holding meetings with a couple of the branch offices."

"You don't have to explain yourself to me, Nick," she replied quietly.

He took his hand off the gear shift and put it on her knee. "Yeah, I do," he said. "I like our dinner dates. I just like spending time with you. Is that so bad?"

"No." She sighed and looked out the window for a few moments. "I'm sorry you had to find out about my job like that."

"I knew it was coming, I just didn't know it was that soon."

"Believe me, neither did I. She told me last week."

"So what are you going to do?"

"I've already rung around but nobody's got back to me." She shrugged. "I have an appointment with the unemployment office next week but they'll probably tell me there's a stand-down."

Nick was silent. Kate had never been one to ask for help and she wasn't about to ask him to help her find a new job, or help her out with money. She still had her pride.

They were both quiet until he pulled into a parking space outside a café. Kate followed him inside and waited as the server greeted them before leading the way to a small table. They'd only been to this café a couple of times and while the staff were friendly, the interior décor wasn't to Kate's liking. She'd always hated the dim lighting in these places, as well as the dark wood panelling which just added to the gloomy ambience.

Nick sat opposite her, his hands clasped in front of him on the table. She bit her lip and looked away from him.

"Katie ..."

"Please don't start, Nick. I don't think I can take anymore."

"Don't start what? Be nice to you? Try to help you? Katie, I know you're independent and you're stubborn as hell, but it doesn't make you weak to ask for help when you need it."

She shook her head. "I'm Irish," she said. "Well, sort of, I guess."

"That doesn't mean anything," he replied. He nudged the menu toward her. "Order something. I don't want you fainting on me."

She picked up the menu and began perusing her choices. Knowing Nick, if she chose the cheapest thing on the menu he was likely to order something else for her, so she decided to go for the meal that appealed to her. It was a simple beef salad but it was good enough for her.

When the server came to take their orders, Nick only ordered a black coffee for himself. She frowned at him. "Aren't you going to order something else?"

"I've already had lunch," he told Kate. "So, anyway, as I was saying, you don't have to be shy about asking for help."

"There aren't any jobs at your company, Nick. I already looked. Where do you think I've been all week? God, I even put in an application at the local fast food places."

His brow furrowed in a deep frown. "Oh no, Katie. You don't want to work in a place like that. For one thing, they pay minimum wage and the hours are horrible."

"Well, what choice do I have? Joy's not going to give me a good reference."

"Oh she bloody well is," he replied, sounding more than a little angry. "Or Mum will have something to say about that. You know, if it wasn't for the fact that her family actually originally owned that building, I'd ..."

Kate put a hand on his, gently squeezing. "You can't. She's on the board too, remember?"

"Still, she has no right to treat you the way she did. Mum doesn't suffer fools gladly and even she says you worked damn hard at that place. Harder than Ms 'I'm so full of myself' Joy Hopkins nee Langston deserved."

Kate giggled. "You just love being a white knight, don't you? I bet you were a real knight in a past life. Not that I'm saying I'm some kind of damsel in distress."

He chuckled, giving her a cheesy grin in return.

"Well, I did always fancy myself as Westley from The Princess Bride when I was a kid."

She snorted. She could just picture him pretending to be the farmhand-turned-pirate, sword in hand, off to save the love of his life. Kate had never been one for fairy tales, preferring stories in which the woman could stand up perfectly well for herself.

A plate was put down in front of her and a coffee cup was placed in front of Nick.

"Can I get you anything else?"

Kate smiled at the woman. "No, thank you. This looks great."

So used to going without lunch and sometimes breakfast, she didn't realise how hungry she was until she began eating. The salad was just as delicious as she had expected and within minutes she had almost cleared her plate. Nick stared at her with an incredulous expression.

"You just wolfed that down like you were starving in the desert!"

She frowned at him. "Huh? That doesn't make any sense."

He shrugged. "I dunno. I heard it somewhere."

"You're weird!"

He wrinkled his nose at her. "Now that's not a nice thing to say to a guy who's buying you lunch."

"Funny, I don't remember asking you to buy me lunch. The only reason I let you is I didn't want to get another lecture."

"You suck," he replied practically throwing her own words from a week ago back in her face.

She couldn't help but laugh. Some people might criticise their relationship but she liked that in spite of his background he didn't put on airs with her. She could tease him without fear that he might take it the wrong way. She'd known others with similar backgrounds who tended to look down on her because she had been raised in a lower-middle-class family.

She'd heard some academics claim that their research didn't support the notion there was a class system in New Zealand, but Kate knew it existed. Hell, she'd lived it. Her parents had worked what amounted to minimum wage jobs and had never really aspired to anything else. Like most families Kate had grown up around, they had always been stuck on the idea that they were born into a certain 'class' and no amount of ambition would ever change that.

That was one thing about Nick's 'proposal' that worried her. While he might not see anything wrong with it, she wondered if others would see her as some kind of opportunist, with one eye on the main chance, so to speak. It was another reason she couldn't accept his help. She didn't want anyone getting the wrong idea and thinking she was sponging off him. The first few times they'd gone out to dinner together, he had practically had to force her not to dig into her purse.

"You know you could go into business for yourself. Why don't you try catering? I mean, you've cooked for me before."

Nick had been in a bind and had asked her to help him with a dinner party. His excuse was that he didn't know how to cook, or at least, not for a dinner party for six. She had written up a menu, taken him shopping for all the food, then cooked it. He'd offered to pay her for her time and she had reluctantly agreed to charge him although he'd told her she was charging too little. She couldn't win with him.

She didn't want to seem like she was giving him excuses but she was nothing if not pragmatic.

"I don't know. It's a lot of work for one person. Besides, where would I get the money to invest in it? I mean, I'd need a vehicle for starters." Then there was rental for a kitchen since there was no way she could cook such meals in her flat. Not to mention the tools she would need. "It's a nice idea, Nick, but not really practical."

"Yeah, guess you're right. I know of a couple of people who do head-hunting for some of the big companies around here. I've already mentioned your name and they said they would look out for you."

She frowned at him. "I'm guessing they weren't very optimistic."

He reached over and squeezed her hand. "I know things look bad, but there's always another option."

She knew exactly what he was talking about.

"Oh no, Nick. We've already talked about this."

"And you haven't given me a real answer."

"I have given you a real answer. I said no."

"Without telling me why."

"Can't you just accept that I said no and drop the subject?"

He grinned, looking unrepentant. "No. You know how stubborn I can be."

She groaned. "Yeah, don't I know it. Honestly, were you like this with your mother growing up?"

"Nope, I was worse."

"Your mother has to have the patience of a saint!"

Kate had met Nick's mother at the gallery when Joy had asked her to host another exhibition opening and the older woman had taken her out for coffee a few times since. She had found Diane Sloane to be a warm and friendly woman who appeared to be under no illusions where her son was concerned.

Nick looked around them. Kate noticed they were putting chairs up on the tables. This was a café that closed up for an hour or two before the dinner crowd. The café also had live music on Friday nights, showcasing local talent.

"Looks like they need to close up," he observed. "Come on."

Kate followed him as he approached the front counter to pay for her meal and his coffee. She made no comment as he took her hand to lead her out of the café. However, instead of going back to his car, he walked with her along the street. There were a couple of fashion boutiques as well as a small, independent bookshop. There was also a small dairy. Kate was puzzled as he pulled her into the convenience store.

"Do you sell phone cards?" he asked the man at the counter.

"What phone?" the shopkeeper asked. He was a young man who appeared to be Asian, although it wasn't obvious where in Asia he was from.

Nick turned to her. "You've got an Azcom phone, right?" She nodded, a little taken aback by the look he shot her. He wasn't going to take any argument from her. He turned back to the man. "Could I have a card loaded for a hundred?"

"Nick …" she began, only for him to squeeze her hand, just hard enough to get his point across.

The man quickly processed the transaction and handed the card over. Nick thanked the storekeeper and led the way back out, along the street to his car.

"Give me your phone," he said. "And don't argue. You need a phone for job interviews."

She sighed and shook her head even as she handed the phone over. "I really hate when you do that," she said, watching as he pressed a few keys on her phone and added the credit.

"I hate when you argue with me. I've told you before. I want to help and this is nothing. Not even a drop in the bucket."

What could she really say to that? she thought. She would just look ungrateful if she kept refusing his help. Still, she wondered why he kept persisting. What was really so special about her?

Chapter Five

Kate left her interview at the unemployment office feeling totally humiliated. It had been almost a month since she'd finished at the gallery and she still hadn't been able to get a new job. Her case manager had told her she wasn't trying hard enough. Wasn't trying hard enough? she thought angrily. She had spent hours pounding the pavement leaving her CV with local businesses, even resorting to trying for work as a waitress in a restaurant. All to no avail. No one had called. Not even leads from Nick had proved fruitful.

The finance company had been curiously silent the past few weeks. It was odd that there hadn't been even one threatening phone call from them. They had always been less than understanding about her financial situation and refused to give her a breather. Their required payment amount was more than half of what she was receiving on the benefit, which meant she would have only been able to pay half her rent and nothing else. She was barely making ends meet as it was.

She walked along the street deep in thought completely oblivious to what was going on around her. She didn't hear the car horn beeping at her or the voice calling her until the car turned into an alleyway and blocked her path.

Diane Sloane smiled and waved at her.

"Goodness, didn't you hear me calling you?" she asked.

Kate shook her head. "Sorry. I was miles away," she said.

"Oh well, that doesn't matter. How about you come and have a coffee with me?"

She bit her lip but nodded before getting in the car. Diane put the vehicle in reverse and planted her foot, ignoring the toots from other drivers as she backed out of the alley. Kate had to grin. Nick's mother was the complete opposite to him in looks - fair where he was dark, but they both seemed to have the same penchant for driving as if they were the only ones on the road.

A few minutes later the older woman pulled into a parking spot, almost hitting the other car in front of her.

"Here we go," she said cheerily. Kate looked at her, then gently reminded her to put the car in park and pull up the handbrake before the car could roll backwards. Diane chuckled at her own absent-mindedness. "Oh dear, I'd forget my head if it wasn't screwed on."

She followed the blonde into a café. The name on the sign said Full o' Beans. A server greeted them with a smile and asked what they would like to order. Diane looked at her.

"What would you like, sweetie?" Her blue-eyes swept over her with a critical gaze. "Hmm, you look almost like skin and bone. Are you eating enough, darling?" She turned back to the server. "Two cappuccinos please. No sugar. We're sweet enough! Oh, and could you perhaps bring us a plate of your delicious scones?"

"Of course Mrs Sloane," the server replied, intimating that Diane was a regular and well-known.

"Mrs Sloane …" Kate began, but the older woman shook her head.

"Diane, please," she said. "How many times must I tell you that?"

"Oh, about a hundred," Kate replied with a mischievous grin. "I'm sure I'll get it one day."

"You'll get something, that's for sure, cheeky miss," Diane returned, chuckling. "Now, let's go find a table." Without waiting for a reply, she turned and headed toward a small round table near the window and sat down. "I love watching people passing by, don't you?"

Kate sat opposite her and put her bag down beside her chair, away from the path between tables. The café wasn't overly full but she preferred to make sure her belongings were secure.

The older woman smiled brightly at her. She was wearing a cream dress which fit her slender figure and suited her complexion. Her blonde hair was cut in a layered bob that was fairly short yet pretty and feminine, suiting her face shape.

"So, tell me what you've been doing with yourself since you left the gallery."

"Um, honestly, just trying to find another job."

Diane frowned in sympathy. "Oh dear, has there been nothing in the offing?"

"Not so far. I've left my CV at a lot of places, but I haven't even had an interview so far."

"Well, that's just not on," the older woman replied. "I know the job situation is terrible at the moment, but really, you'd think these people would recognise a young woman with such skills as yours."

"You'd think so," Kate told her. She didn't want to voice her suspicions that Joy had given her a bad reference, even though Nick had told her he would make sure her former boss wouldn't.

The server approached their table with their coffees and the scones. She had supplied them with a plate of butter and jam as well as a little bowl of whipped cream. Diane beamed at the server.

"You are an angel," she said. "Thank you very much."

"You're welcome," the girl replied with a wide smile. She was a pretty girl with Asian features and spoke English with no discernible accent. Kate noticed the girl was wearing a name tag that said: 'Jing'.

Diane chatted with the girl, asking after her family and how school was going. Kate gleaned from the conversation that Jing was at university full-time and worked part-time in the café. The tone of the conversation was friendly, giving even more of an impression that Diane was a regular customer who took a motherly interest in the girls working there. The staff didn't appear to mind at all.

More customers came in and Diane reluctantly let Jing go attend to them, turning back to Kate.

"Sweetie, why aren't you eating?"

"I was waiting for you," Kate told her politely.

The older woman waved her hand. "Oh, don't worry about me. Eat, darling, please."

Kate usually didn't like being called pet names by people who weren't family but for as long as she'd known Nick's mother, she'd been called 'sweetie' or 'darling' and it had seemed sweet rather than overbearing.

She obeyed her companion and helped herself to a scone, adding jam and whipped cream. Diane smiled at her, her expression showing satisfaction as Kate bit into the scone.

"So, tell me what's been going on between you and my son," she said.

Kate almost choked on the bite of food. She wondered if Nick had been telling his mother about his so-called proposal. He'd asked her again four more times since her last day at the gallery. She'd always known he could be persistent, but it was getting a little ridiculous.

"Why? What has he been saying?"

"Oh, nothing much," Diane said airily. "He just tells me he's been offering to help you with your job-hunting and your financial situation but you keep turning him down."

She sighed, a little relieved that that was all he'd been saying.

"I don't know. I guess I'm just used to handling it by myself. I've been on my own since my parents died."

She didn't talk about what had happened to her parents. When she had been studying for her degree at university, they had all lived in an old bungalow which had needed serious renovations. Kate had been asleep when some faulty wiring had shorted out in her parents' bedroom, causing a fire which had engulfed the bungalow in minutes. Kate had just barely got out herself and emergency workers had told her that her parents had more than likely never woken up. She'd lost everything in the fire and there had been no insurance.

The property's owner had never bothered to install smoke detectors or any kind of warning system, so Kate considered herself lucky to have been able to escape the fire at all.

The other woman nodded. "You know, I was very like you when Nick was little. His father walked out when he was a toddler. I was so sure I could handle it all by myself, but I'm afraid I got myself into rather a bit of a mess. Of course, I didn't have financial difficulties but let me tell you that that was the least of my problems. How do you explain to a little boy that his father wasn't coming back? The tantrums my boy had; I was just about at the end of my tether, I tell you. I really didn't know what to do."

"So, what happened?" Kate asked. She'd never heard this story before and was fascinated by the thought that the usually together woman had had problems coping.

"Well, I eventually found some other women in the same situation and they helped me. Not that I'm saying that it's anything similar to your situation but I learnt to ask for help. Sometimes being independent is not a good thing."

"I don't want to be a burden," she said.

Diane frowned at her. "Can I ask you a question? Kind of a personal one?"

She shrugged. "I guess."

"Do you think you're not worth it?"

She looked at the older woman, a little confused by the question. "What?"

"Well, honey, you care about Nick, don't you? I see the way you look at him sometimes."

She opened her mouth, worried that Diane had said something to her son, or that Nick might have talked to her about the proposal after all, but the older woman waved her hand.

"Oh trust me, my son can be really dense at times and he doesn't know a thing. What I'm trying to say is, you're a wonderful young woman. You're kind and sensitive and you make my boy laugh. I know you've had a hard life, sweetie, but I've watched you when you've been with him and I think he's as good for you as you are for him. So why do you think you don't deserve him?"

"It's not ... I worry about what other people might say," she confessed. Diane nodded. She obviously understood it from Kate's point of view but her expression suggested she considered that irrelevant.

"Well, darling, at the end of the day, it's not really what other people say that matters. You know, someone once told me something a long time ago. You can't please everyone. Half of the people you know are only going to like you half of the time. And please don't take this the wrong way because you know I love you to bits, but you can be far too hard on yourself sometimes. Nick's talked about some of the things you've told him, about your family, and let me tell you, your great-grandfather, who I'm sure was a decent man, was wrong. About a lot of things. Yes, it takes hard work and you know how hard my Nicky works at his job, but not everything has to be a battle. Your grandfather, bless his heart, lived in a very hard time but that doesn't mean he knew everything about the way the world works."

Diane drank the last of her coffee and gazed at her, her blue eyes thoughtful.

"Do you know why I decided to support the gallery?"

Kate nodded. "Nick told me. You had a cousin or something who was an artist."

The other woman's nod echoed hers. "His father told him he didn't have a lick of talent and should get a normal job, like painting and plastering. Do you know what I told him? If it's your dream, then who cares what other people think? And you know, maybe he's never made much money but he makes enough to live on his own terms and that's all that matters."

It wasn't as if Kate had always dreamed of working as an administrator. When she was young she had wanted to work in a museum. She loved anything to do with history and wanted to be like the curator at the local museum who took schoolchildren on tours through the museum, telling stories about the people who had lived more than a hundred years ago.

Still, she needed a post-graduate diploma in museum studies to at least be considered and she couldn't afford to go back to university. Diane smiled at her.

"I know that look. Tell me."

"When I was a kid I wanted to be a museum curator," she said.

"What's stopping you?" the other woman asked.

"I would need to study a post-grad diploma for one and two, there aren't that many job opportunities."

"Well, yes, you're right about the job opportunities, but there's nothing wrong with talking to the right people. I happen to know someone who knows someone on the museum's board. How's your Maori language?"

Kate grimaced. "Ahh, not so good. I took a paper at uni but I haven't been able to practice it since."

"You're a smart girl. I'm sure you'd pick it up." She glanced at the watch on her wrist. It looked fairly old, with what Kate guessed was tiny cubic zirconia stones embedded around the watch face. The bracelet was also decorated with the little stones, then held together with a narrow chain. "Goodness, look at the time. I should get going. Nick's coming to dinner and I need to get to the supermarket. Why don't you come too, Kate? You need fattening up."

Kate laughed and agreed to come. She hadn't seen Nick in a couple of weeks as he'd been busy with negotiations on a new acquisition.

Diane dropped her off by the driveway and waved as she drove off, barely avoiding a car coming the other way. Kate was left shaking her head in fond exasperation at Nick's mother.

Out of habit, she checked the letterbox before heading down the path to her door and was surprised to find two letters addressed to her. The letterbox was shared between all five flats and she very rarely found mail for her. Kate opened one of the letters as she walked, staring in shock at the official letter. At the top, the return address was for a lawyer with the Financial Authority, a government agency given powers to regulate finance companies.

Dear Miss Delaney,

We are writing to advise you that your account with Finance Assist has been suspended due to an investigation by our office into their practices. Please suspend any and all future payments to this company until this matter is resolved.

She stared at the words in the letter. Investigation? Nick, she thought. It had to be. It was no wonder then that the company hadn't contacted her asking about their payments.

She opened the door of her flat and dumped her keys on the counter before opening the other letter, which was from her landlord. It looked like a copy of a letter distributed to all the tenants as it was all typed except for her name, which was written in blue ink.

Dear Kate,

We regret to inform you that your flat, as have all the flats in the building, has been bought by a private investor. We're sorry to spring this on you, but the offer came out of the blue and we couldn't pass it up. The contract will be final in about thirty days. We believe the investor is planning on tearing the old house down and rebuilding, so please regard this as your notice to vacate.

The letter went on to say that the owner would follow the letter of the law with the tenancy, giving her just over a month to find another place. It was a little unusual for someone who had cared so little about the tenants' welfare that they had barely done any maintenance the whole time she had lived in the place.

Kate sat down on the lumpy sofa bed, reading the notice over and over. How could they do this to her, she thought. Where was she supposed to go? Flats with as cheap a rent as hers were very hard to come by.

Chapter Six

Nick sent her a text telling her he would pick her up and take her to his mother's place for dinner. She considered texting him back telling him not to but figured he wouldn't take no for an answer anyway.

She quickly showered and dressed in a pretty skirt and blouse. Both were a little worn but they would do. She was ready to go by the time Nick knocked on her door, grabbing her bag and keys on her way out.

She glanced at the car as he threw her bag in the back. It was a Series 3 BMW. He'd obviously decided to splash out a bit as the car still had that new leather smell. It wasn't a flash car by any means. Nick had often told her he preferred to buy vehicles that were comfortable rather than aesthetically pleasing yet also stood the test of his driving. Not that he was a bad driver, per se, just a little hard on his vehicles sometimes.

"How's the job hunting going?" he asked as he drove off. She shrugged.

"Same as usual. No one even deigns to reply."

He reached between the seats to squeeze her hand but she pulled away.

"What's wrong?" he asked.

She bit her lip. She didn't want to get in a fight with him over the finance company or accuse him without having all the facts. Not now, at least. Diane was far too astute not to notice any tension between them.

"It's nothing," she said. "I'm just tired. I had an interview at the unemployment office today and the case manager told me I wasn't trying hard enough to get a job. Like I haven't been walking the streets and giving every Tom, Dick, and Harry my CV."

"I'm sorry," he said. "That must hurt."

"Story of my life," she replied with a sigh. "Please don't say anything to your mum. You know how she worries."

"She likes you," Nick told her. "She wouldn't worry so much about you if she didn't like you.

She tried for a weak smile. "Well, the feeling is mutual." She studied him. He looked a little tired. "How's work?"

"Exhausting," he said. "I've been working until almost ten every night for the past couple of weeks trying to negotiate this acquisition. The owner of the company we're looking to buy-out is being rather stubborn." He glanced at her, cocking an eyebrow. "Sure he's not a relation of yours?"

"Ha ha," she responded dryly.

"Seriously though, he keeps coming back wanting to change things in the contract."

"What's so special about the company?"

"It's not so much that it's special. The owner's an old man. He wants to retire up north, spend time with his grandkids. His family's not interested in taking over the business. I guess he's just being difficult because it's so hard to let go."

"I can understand that," she said quietly.

"Yeah, me too." He was silent for a few moments as he negotiated a sharp turn. His mother had a house about fifteen minutes' drive from the city in a town small enough to be considered more or less a village. While she was very social, she often said she liked the quiet locale.

"Listen," Nick began, "I was thinking. This weekend, I was going to take a drive. Maybe up north. Spend the weekend at the lake. Perry has a bach there. Do you want to come with me? There's a spare bedroom if you're worried."

She looked at him. His face was guileless, suggesting he wasn't planning anything except taking time out to relax. She could certainly do with a break away and since it was a holiday on Monday, she doubted she would be contacted for any interviews.

"Okay," she said.

He looked surprised at her quick acquiescence but didn't comment while looking out for his mother's driveway. Diane Sloane lived in a fairly large house that she had inherited from her parents. It was almost too large for a woman on her own, but it had been in the family for at least three generations.

The house itself was probably about one hundred years old but unlike the house Kate's flat was part of, Diane's was well-maintained. She had had some renovations done about a year before Kate had met Nick and was always boasting about her kitchen. While she had modernised, she'd been careful to ensure it was still in keeping with the rest of the house.

The grounds themselves were landscaped. Diane was a keen gardener and loved, as she called it, pottering about, tending to her flowers.

She must have heard the car approaching as she stepped out to meet them while Nick parked the car. She kissed her son's cheek and hugged Kate.

"Come in," she said. She glanced at Nick. "Darling, you look exhausted. Are you not sleeping?" she enquired.

"Too many late nights," he responded. His mother tsked.

"Now what have I told you about working too much."

"You know I try to have a work-life balance, Mum," he said, half-laughing at the way she fussed over him as she led them inside. "But sometimes it happens."

They sat on bar stools at the marble-topped counter. It had been expensive, but Diane had loved the patterns. She had spared no expense in the renovation, turning the kitchen into what she called an entertainer's dream. She loved to cook for guests.

Kate watched as Diane checked on dinner, then continued chattering as she stood behind the counter.

"Nonsense. No company is worth losing sleep over. Now, would you like a wine?" She pursed her lips at Nick. "Hmm, no, I think it'll be just orange juice for you, darling. You shouldn't drink alcohol when you're that tired."

"Yes Mum," he said with a grin.

Kate couldn't help chuckling as she listened to the chatter between mother and son. Nick hated being fussed over but he clearly loved his mother dearly and put up with it simply because she was his mother.

Of course, once Diane was done fussing over her son, it was Kate's turn. The older woman clucked, implying she was not happy at Kate's slender figure.

"She's too skinny, don't you think so Nicky?"

"She looks fine to me, Mum."

Diane practically rolled her eyes at him. "You're like all men, Nicky. You never notice anything unless it's pointed out to you. You haven't even commented on my haircut."

Oops, Kate thought with a grin at Nick. At least she had an excuse since it had been a couple of months since she had seen Diane.

"I got it done at this new hairdresser in town. The lady did a wonderful job. Don't you think so?" the older woman said, patting her hair carefully. It did look good, Kate thought.

"It looks great, Mum," Nick said dutifully.

"It suits you," Kate added. Diane smiled at her.

"Thank you, darling. I know I can always count on you."

The oven timer dinged, signalling dinner was ready. Diane had made a lasagne with steamed vegetables on the side. They sat at the table with their meals. Nick had piled his plate high with the vegetables. Diane watched her son with almost an eagle-eyed gaze.

"You know, when you were three you would scream if I left even one vegetable on your plate," she commented.

"I did not, Mum," he said, rolling his eyes. He shook his head at Kate. "She's exaggerating."

His mother huffed loudly. "Am I now? I remember you having a fit when I accidentally gave you a little tiny piece of carrot."

Nick scowled at her. "Don't go telling Kate tall tales. She'd run a mile if you keep that up."

"I have yet to show her the bare-bottom shots I have of you when you were just barely walking."

He groaned. "Mum! You're embarrassing me!"

"Perish the thought," Kate commented, earning a dirty look from him for her trouble. He wrinkled his nose at her.

"You'll keep," he said.

"That a promise or a threat?" she returned, laughing at his put-upon expression. He turned to his mother.

"See what I have to put up with?"

"Oh, you poor baby!" Diane responded. Kate couldn't resist teasing him further.

"Let me get out my violin," she added.

He glowered at her but had clearly decided the more he protested the worse it would get so he turned back to his meal.

Kate enjoyed the dinner and the company, feeling pleasantly tired by the time Nick dropped her off home. It wasn't until she saw the letter on the counter as she was getting ready for bed that she realised she had forgotten all about talking to Nick about it.

He picked her up late the next afternoon. He had planned to drive north to the lakeside town that night so they would have at least two full days at the bach. The journey would take around three hours and included a fifty-kilometre journey through land which the local army base used for training. While it was called the Desert Road, it didn't really resemble the desert as Kate would have expected from seeing images of an actual desert. The land was dotted with various vegetation the training soldiers often used to camouflage themselves during exercises.

The road also had a winding area which ran for about twenty kilometres. This part also took them past the volcanic plateau and the three most famous volcanoes in the entire country. Kate often reflected on the beauty of the mountains which belied their potentially deadly nature.

She was always relieved when the vehicle she was in emerged the other side unscathed. There had been numerous car accidents in which there had been fatalities in the area, a large percentage of them due to harsh weather conditions. The volcanic plateau was one of the few areas in the North Island where the authorities often had to close the road in winter due to snow.

They didn't talk much on the journey. Nick had obviously downloaded some music he knew she liked and played them on the MP3 player. Kate found herself drifting off a little even with the music.

It was dark when they arrived at the lakeside township. Kate sleepily watched as Nick drove up a side street and turned into a narrow driveway and parked the car beneath a carport. He grabbed their bags from the back and led the way inside. The bach was fairly small and clearly only suited for short stays, as were most of the cottages near the lake.

Kate's room was again small, with only a single bed, but she was too tired to care. Considering the old sofa bed she normally slept on, an actual mattress was going to be bliss. She dumped her bag on the floor, intending to unpack a little later.

"You hungry?" Nick called out from the other room.

"Yeah, I could do with something to eat."

"How about I order some fish and chips? There's a shop near the waterfront that delivers."

"Sounds good," she said, grabbing her bag and pulling out a hooded sweatshirt. It had been a warm day back home but here a cold wind was blowing up from the lake.

She went out to find Nick on the phone, calling in the order. He looked up and smiled at her before confirming the order then hung up the phone.

"All sorted," he said.

"Okay. Good."

He patted the couch. "I'm really glad you came with me," he said. "I wanted to talk to you."

"You're not going to want to talk about that thing that we don't talk about, are you?" she asked, moving to join him.

"Well, yeah. I mean … Look, I know we can make this work, Katie. We get along so well together. We share a few laughs."

"That's hardly a basis for marriage."

"But it's a good starting point, isn't it?" He seemed so earnest, she almost forgot she was still a little upset with him.

"Is it?" she asked, remembering the letter she'd received. "So is honesty."

He frowned at her. "What do you mean?"

She took a deep breath. "I got a letter yesterday. Actually a couple of them. One was from the Financial Authority telling me that the finance company I'm still paying money to is under investigation. You wouldn't know anything about that, would you?"

He looked at her sombrely. "I made a couple of calls, yeah."

"Why?"

"Because what they did to you was fraud, Katie. Your ex took out that loan and signed your name without your knowledge or consent. They should never have accepted the contract."

She shook her head. She'd tried to tell the company that early on when she'd learnt about the loan, but they hadn't wanted to know.

"You're not the only one they've done it to," he said. "I'm sorry if you think I went behind your back, but what they did wasn't right. Do you know exactly how much you've paid them?"

She shrugged. She'd lost count.

"The original loan was for a few thousand. You've paid them ...What? A hundred a week for how long? Five years? That's over twenty-five thousand dollars, Katie. You've paid the loan at least twice over."

"There's interest," she pointed out.

"Even at a high finance rate, it's never that much. Think about it. Do the maths. You know I'm right."

She considered it, then realised he was right. The finance company had taken far more than they should have. She was an idiot. An utter fool for letting it go that long.

"Someone had to stand up for you and the countless others they've robbed, Katie. These people are loan sharks. What they've done is illegal."

"You're right. I'm sorry." He studied her.

"That's what you were upset about last night, wasn't it?"

She nodded. "Yeah."

"I knew there was something. Katie, I was just trying to look out for you."

"I get that now. It's just ... you know how sometimes you try your hardest but no matter what you do you just can't seem to get anywhere? Then someone comes along and it seems so easy for them."

He shook his head. "You know it's not that easy. I have to work just as hard as you to get what I want. I guess I never told you this, but when I was at uni, I had this professor. He knew my mother and would often criticise me, thinking that I would never take my studies seriously because I came from a fairly wealthy background. Like I could buy my degree. I had to work damn hard to prove to him that I wasn't just some empty-headed layabout who cared more about partying than I did about studying. It's where I also learnt some valuable lessons about knowing when to stop working. My third year at uni I was studying about ten papers and I was this close to a burnout," he said, holding up his thumb and forefinger, keeping them just a centimetre apart.

She knew it wasn't easy for him either but his story had shown her just how hard it was for him to prove that he was more than his family's wealth. People could be so judgmental, she thought. Even herself.

Nick got up to answer the knock on the door and took the food from the delivery person. Kate could smell the delicious aroma of fresh, battered fish and salty chips. Her stomach rumbled, reminding her she hadn't eaten much that day, except for an apple in the car. They ate in companionable silence.

The next morning dawned bright and sunny and Kate decided to walk along the waterfront. Nick opted to join her. They walked for a little while, then sat on one of the benches, watching people in boats training on the lake.

"My flat's going to be torn down," she told Nick.

He looked at her. "When?"

"I don't know. The landlord got an offer and the new owner wants to tear the place down. I've got a month to find a new place."

"You could move in with me," he said.

"Nick, come on. Please, not the marriage thing again."

Nick sighed heavily.

"Why do you keep turning me down?" he asked. "I'm offering you a way to solve your problems."

"By getting married!" she pointed out.

He shrugged. "Well, why not?"

"Why not? Nick, when or if I ever get married, I want it to be for love. Not to solve my financial problems."

"Love? Come on, Katie."

"No, you come on. I mean, what on Earth would we tell people? We're not in love."

"Why is that so important to you? I mean, think about it. How many people get married to the person who is supposedly the love of their lives, only for it to come crashing down around them? Look at Perry. He's been down the aisle twice and is working on his third. How long do you think that will last?"

"Perry can't help flirting with every woman in sight. It's no wonder his first two marriages failed. They couldn't trust him!"

He nodded as if to concede the point.

"Okay, bad example. What about my mum then? She got married for love and look what happened. She ended up a single mother with a kid and I ended up with a deadbeat dad."

"He's not a deadbeat dad," Kate told him in protest. He raised an eyebrow at her. "I mean, he would have to actually be a dad to be a deadbeat dad, wouldn't he?"

"Good point." Nick got up from the bench and stood by the fence, watching the activity on the lake for a few moments. He ran a hand through his hair, tousling it. "The thing is, I …" He looked at her sheepishly. "I forgot the point I was trying to make."

"You wanted to know why love was so important to me."

"Yeah, that's it."

She got up to join him, watching the waves crash on the shore. While it was sunny, the breeze coming off the water was cold and she shivered. Nick held her, stroking her bare arms. She averted her gaze, sighing.

"I just … I don't know. If I ever do get married, I want it to be … you know, for good. Death do us part and all that. I want it to be real."

"Who says that what I'm offering isn't going to be a real marriage," he told her. "I mean, you're the one who used the phrase marriage of convenience. If I recall correctly, I told you my reasons for getting married was so I could give my mother grand-children." He looked seriously at her. "Would it really be that much of a hardship to be married to me?"

It wouldn't be a hardship, she thought, except for the fact that he didn't love her. What if he met someone and fell in love? Surely he'd want to divorce her to marry the woman he loved? What would she do then? Marrying him, only to have him leave her for someone else would break her heart.

"Katie?"

"No," she said quietly. "I mean, no, it wouldn't be a hardship, but …"

"But what? If it's a problem being convincing to our friends, not to mention Mum, well, I can solve that."

How? she was about to ask when he pressed his lips to hers. It probably wasn't the greatest of kisses considering he had taken her by surprise, but Kate found herself responding to his gentle coaxing. He explored her mouth, almost tentatively, as if trying to map every contour.

When they broke apart, Kate realised that somehow her arms had found their way around his neck, while he had wrapped his arms around her waist. She dropped her arms, staring at him in a 'deer in the headlights' manner.

Nick frowned. "You're looking at me like I suddenly grew another head or something." He shook his head. "Yeah, that was terrible. Let's try that again."

Kate was a little more prepared this time as he pulled her closer and tilted her chin so he could press his mouth to hers. She clung to him as the kiss set her body almost on fire. His tongue probed her mouth in such a way as to claim ownership, his body pressing so close she could feel his muscles rippling with every movement.

The embrace was intoxicating. She breathed in the scent of him, her senses concentrated only on the way he smelled like fresh air. She wanted more, her body almost begging to be claimed in a way she couldn't remember ever feeling with any other man she'd dated.

It felt as if she was being branded as his hands caressed her back, her skin tingling at his touch.

Again she found herself staring at him when he stepped back. She was inexplicably breathless as if she had run a cross-country race. Her face was hot and she pressed cool hands to her cheeks.

God, if this was what his kisses could do to her … How could she let this man go? she thought.

"Okay, Nick," she said. "You win."

He seemed a little dazed as he bent his head and murmured.

"Win what?"

"I'll marry you."

Chapter Seven

Once the decision was made, Nick was full of plans. Like when, how and where they would get married. From the way he kept talking about it, it seemed almost like a coronation rather than just a simple wedding. Kate had never really given much thought to what kind of ceremony she would like.

She didn't want to get caught up in his enthusiasm but her new fiancé, and didn't that give her an odd tingly feeling, was like a kid in a candy store. As soon as they got back to the bach, he grabbed his laptop and began researching online. He was booking a wedding planner before she'd even had a chance to object.

"Nick, slow down," she said in protest.

He looked at her. "Oh hell no. I'm not giving you a chance to change your mind. I mean, look at how long it took you to actually say yes."

"That's not the point. And anyway, is that really what you think I'll do? Once I've made a promise, I don't go back on my word. You know I don't do that."

He wrapped an arm around her shoulders and squeezed. "Yeah, I know. But I'm still going to make damn sure you can't get away." He turned back to his computer. "So, we should have a party. To celebrate our engagement."

"A party?" she asked faintly. A party, where he was likely to invite friends from work as well as his mother. Kate didn't have any friends she could invite. She had had a small circle of friends when she had spent a year or so living in a small community about a hundred or so kilometres south of the city, but none of them were people she would have considered to be close friends. She had a second cousin she was fairly close to and one very close friend but doubted her friend would fit in with any of Nick's circle. Teri had come from a similar background to her and in many ways was more sensitive than Kate. Nick's friends, nice though some of them were, would eat her for breakfast, lunch, and dinner.

Nick at least listened to her on one point. She had asked him not to send in an announcement to the local media and not to say anything on Facebook or any of the other social media sites he used online. He agreed, on the condition that they would make the announcement together at the engagement party.

The way he practically leapt into organising everything made Kate feel like she'd been run over by a steamroller. It occurred to her to wonder why this marriage was so important to him but didn't ask him about it. She was just glad that he was happy with her decision.

If she was being honest with herself, she was just as happy, even if she was also very nervous about what was ahead for them. Nick was making it very clear that this not going to be a marriage of convenience the way she pictured it. He wanted a real marriage, with children.

On the drive back on Monday, Nick asked her to move in with him.

"Nick …"

"Come on, I mean, what's your landlord going to do if you move out early? He's already given you notice."

"I can't just move in with you."

"Well, you'll have to in six weeks," he replied. "I mean, it's hardly practical to move into another place when you'll be living with me in three months."

They'd decided on a wedding date in January, just over three months away. Kate had wanted to wait longer, while Nick had wanted an earlier date, so they'd compromised and chosen a date somewhere in between.

She relented. "Nick, I understand that. I do. It's just … this is all just moving a little too fast for me. We only just got engaged."

He smiled softly at her, then leaned over and kissed her cheek. "You're right. I'm being pushy." He pulled up beside her driveway. "So I'll call you later in the week, okay?"

She nodded, wondering if she should kiss him back. He answered that for her with a quick kiss on the mouth. Kate frowned, her lips tingling from his kiss. Nick got out of the car and grabbed her bag from the boot, then helped her out of the car. Not that she needed it.

She watched him drive off, wondering what she had got herself into.

As promised, Nick did call her later in the week, but his tone was distracted.

"Is everything okay?" she asked tentatively.

"Yeah. Just that negotiation I was telling you about last week. It's giving me a headache."

She was tempted to go over to his place and see what she could do to alleviate his tension. He sounded completely stressed.

"Don't worry about me," he assured her when she asked him about it. "I'm a big boy."

Still, they were getting married, she thought as she ended the call. Maybe he was only marrying her to help her out financially, but she should at least return the favour, so to speak.

Having made up her mind, Kate grabbed her bag and a light jacket, then left the flat. It was a short walk to the supermarket. Within about half an hour she had loaded her trolley with fresh vegetables and some fresh meat as well as a bottle of wine she knew Nick liked.

Nick had given her some cash to buy herself some decent food, refusing to let his fiancée survive on just soup and toast. She had had a lot of practice in buying food on a budget and knew she'd be able to make the funds stretch if necessary. However, Nick was used to food that was more expensive than what she usually bought and the cost of the groceries at the end of her shopping trip made her wince.

She called for a taxi on the supermarket's courtesy phone and waited outside for it. The car didn't take that long to arrive and she was swiftly on her way to Nick's townhouse in one of the more affluent parts of the city.

Kate had been to the home a few times and had always admired it, thinking one day she would like to own something similar. The house was about five years old. Nick had bought a house and land package from a local construction company and had chosen a very modern design. It was split-level, with a huge living area which opened out into a beautifully landscaped private courtyard where Nick and his guests could sit and eat without fear of being spied on.

There were three fairly large bedrooms upstairs, all lavishly decorated in a mix of dark and light tones. Kate loved the master bedroom the best as Nick had gone for furniture in a colour which brought out the natural tones of the wood. While the style was still fairly modern, Nick had once told her he preferred natural materials rather than synthetic.

He'd given her a key to the house during their weekend at the lake. While he hadn't said anything, Kate had assumed he had wanted her to start bringing some of her stuff over - not that she had much. She used the key to let herself in, noting as she did so that the house was dark.

She put her bags down and went to inspect the kitchen. When she had helped him with the dinner party she had loved working in the huge space. The kitchen was fairly large with a marble-topped counter in the middle where she could chop up vegetables without turning her back on any guests.

Kate checked the fridge and the freezer and as she suspected there was no fresh food. Nick might scold her for her eating habits but when he was caught up in work he would forget to buy groceries. Since he'd been working late for much of the past two or three weeks it looked like he hadn't been shopping at all in that time.

She opened the chiller to find several vegetables which had started to turn brown. There were other items that she noticed were already moulding. Grimacing, she pulled them out and threw them away.

"What are you doing?"

Startled, Kate whirled and stared at Nick, a hand on her chest.

"Geez, don't do that. You gave me a fright. I didn't even hear you come in."

He had obviously seen the bags she'd left in the foyer as he put them on the counter.

"I repeat. What are you doing?"

"Cleaning out your chiller. You've got stuff in there that should have been thrown out days ago."

He shrugged. "I haven't had time to do much of anything." He ran a hand through his hair and groaned.

Kate looked him over. He had dark shadows under his eyes and his face was pale.

"You look tired," she said sympathetically.

"Yeah. Rough week." He leaned heavily on the counter. "Um, don't think I'm not happy to see you, but why are you here?"

"I thought you could use a decent meal," she said. "And I figured you would be too tired to cook something."

"I was going to order a pizza or something."

She shook her head. "Pizza? That's not healthy."

He shrugged again. Kate shook her head at him and began rummaging in the plastic bags for the food. He seemed to perk up a little bit as she pulled out the steaks she'd bought.

"I thought I'd cook a couple of steaks and make a salad," she said. "It's nothing fancy, but …"

"You don't have to do this," he said, watching as she took the steaks from the pack and placed them on a board to tenderise them before rubbing them with crushed peppercorns. She put them in the fridge to chill for a few minutes then turned back to him.

"Nick, if we're getting married, then …"

"Don't you mean when we get married?"

"Okay, fine. When. The point is, you're the one who said you want this to be a 'real' marriage and well, in my mind a real marriage is a partnership. You take care of me and I take care of you. It's called reciprocity."

"Reciprocity?" he said, raising an eyebrow. She just knew he was about to say something smart.

"Don't even think about it," she warned.

"Think about what?" he returned with a cheeky grin. "Anyway, that's not what I meant. I didn't ask you to marry me so you could become my housekeeper. I can cook you know."

She looked steadily at him. "Well, knowing your mum, she would never have let you move out without at least knowing the basics. But I know you, Nick. When you get caught up in work you forget to eat."

He looked as if he was going to argue, then clearly thought better of it.

"Okay, you're right. I've been so busy I haven't taken the time to eat." He straightened up. "So, what do you want me to do?"

"Nothing except go have a nice, long, hot shower. It'll probably take about half an hour to cook these steaks."

He frowned. "Are you sure there's nothing I can …"

She waved her hand at him. "Shoo!"

She watched him go before returning her attention to making the salad, washing and chopping up the vegetables and putting them in a salad bowl.

Nick appeared about twenty minutes later looking a lot more refreshed. Kate had already poured a couple of glasses of wine from the bottle she'd bought and left one on the counter for him. He sat on one of the stools and watched as she worked, frying the steaks in a deep frypan on the gas hob.

"Feel better?" she asked.

"A little," he replied, then grimaced, rubbing the back of his neck. "Wish I could get rid of this headache though."

She frowned at him. "Is it bad?"

"It's just a migraine," he said. "It's nothing."

She shook her head. She knew he experienced migraine headaches infrequently although they tended to occur more often when he was working too many hours. He'd once told her that he had had to learn the hard way that all work and no play, rather than make him 'a very dull boy' as the saying went, could have a detrimental effect on his health. Most of the time, he kept reasonable hours and tried to exercise at least half an hour a day, but there were times when it just wasn't possible. That coupled with him skipping meals and he became more susceptible to the migraines which had plagued him through his adolescence.

He usually tried to downplay them, like he was doing now as if they weren't that serious. Kate chose not to comment, knowing he was just stubborn enough to pretend he was fine when he wasn't.

She served up the steaks and took the salad bowl to the table, letting Nick help himself. He cut into his meat and beamed at her.

"Cooked to perfection. I think I'll keep you on."

She rolled her eyes at him. "Funny guy."

"Seriously, this is great. Thank you."

After they'd eaten, she once again shooed him out, telling him to go relax in front of the television while she cleaned the kitchen. She heard what sounded like commentary for a rugby game and guessed he'd turned on the sports channel.

She went out to join him once she'd cleaned up and sat in the armchair, pretending to be interested in the game.

"I can put on something else if you don't like it," he suggested after a while, then switched over to the movie channel without waiting for an answer.

It wasn't that she didn't like watching sports games. Nick had once invited her to a rugby match being played at the stadium. Several of his friends had also bought tickets. Kate had been caught up in the excitement as the game progressed, feeling it was different being at an actual live game rather than watching it on television. She didn't understand much about rugby but she could still get an idea of what was happening by the reactions of the people around her.

She curled up in the armchair, glancing occasionally at Nick as a romantic comedy played out on the screen. He was stretched out on the couch, his feet up, a pillow beneath his head. She could see his eyes were drooping but he was fighting the drowsiness. It was fairly obvious that he had been having one too many late nights and it was catching up with him.

The gentle snore a short while later told her he had fallen asleep. Kate got up quietly and went out, grabbing a blanket from the linen cupboard in the hallway. She draped it gently over his sleeping form and switched off the television. Nick snorted but didn't wake.

She leaned over and softly kissed his lips. "Goodnight." She tiptoed out, picking up her bag and quietly left the house.

Chapter Eight

"Katie?"

She heard Nick's knock before the squeaking hinges told her he'd walked right in. She shut off the water and wrapped a towel around her head. Her shower hadn't been working and she had to resort to washing her hair with a small jug in the bathroom sink.

"What are you doing?" he asked as she went out to greet him.

"Washing my hair," she replied irritably. "What does it look like?"

"Oh, duh! Guess I should have known from the turban on your head."

"What do you want, Nick?" she said with a sigh. "We weren't supposed to be meeting until the party tomorrow."

"Uh, yeah, about that. Um, what are you wearing?"

She looked down at the tank top and yoga pants she was wearing. She always wore them around home as they were comfortable.

"Clothes."

"I meant for the party tomorrow, idiot!"

He was clearly feeling better. It had been a couple of days since she had cooked dinner for him. He hadn't said anything about the way she had left him asleep on the couch and she hadn't mentioned it.

It was obvious from the colour in his cheeks and the way he seemed so energetic that he had been able to catch up on his sleep. His eyes twinkled as he looked at her expectantly.

"Um, I was just gonna wear a skirt and top."

Nick frowned at her, then gestured toward the rail where she kept her clothes.

"Show me."

Kate hadn't exactly planned her outfit for their engagement party, but she figured she could just pick out anything that would at least be semi-formal. It was supposed to be a dinner party.

She sifted through the clothes and picked out a black velvet skirt with a forest green blouse which she usually wore for job interviews. She'd found it in the local second-hand clothing store. It had been a bargain at just five dollars for the whole outfit and she wasn't going to complain about the musty smell. Or the tiny rip in the skirt. Both problems had been easily fixed.

Nick eyed the outfit critically, then shook his head. "Nope. That's not gonna do."

Kate bit her lip. "Well, there's that grey dress I wore at the opening of Perry's exhibition."

The dress was in a zipper bag she stored on the shelf above the two cupboards over the little grill.

Nick scowled. "That rag? Didn't Joy give you that dress?"

"Uh, yeah."

He shook his head again. "Nope, that won't do either. For one thing, it was totally shapeless. I mean, the only worse thing she could have done was hand you a sack. What was she thinking?" He huffed. "Actually, I know what she was thinking. She was totally jealous because you're way prettier than she is. I've always thought she was threatened by you."

He shrugged his shoulders. Kate stared at him, wondering if he was right about her former boss. There had certainly been times when she'd thought Joy hated her for some reason.

"Anyway, that dress was totally wrong for you."

He started going through her clothes, shoving things aside with a deep frown on his face, muttering to himself.

"Don't you have anything nice?" he asked, turning to look at her.

"What's wrong with my clothes?" she responded, feeling a little defensive. She'd done her best to choose clothes that at least looked nice, even if they were nothing fancy. There weren't really a lot of options in second-hand clothing stores.

"Nothing, if you want to look like your average plain Jane, which by the way, you are definitely not." He sighed deeply. "Nothing for it. Go dry your hair. We're going shopping!"

"What? Nick!"

He patted her backside and practically shoved her in the direction of the little bathroom.

"Don't argue. We needed to go get a ring anyway. Can't have people thinking this isn't the real deal."

"But it's not ..." she began, but he pointed his finger in the direction of the bathroom.

"What did I just say? Go!"

She glowered at him. "Has anyone told you you're bossy?"

"How do you think I got to be where I am," he replied, grinning unrepentantly.

Growling to herself, Kate went into the bathroom and pulled the towel off, doing her best to get most of the dampness out of her long hair. She grabbed her brush and began working all the knots out. By the time she was done, the curls were reasonably smooth, but her hair was still damp.

Nick came in. "Don't you have a hair dryer?" he asked.

She shot him a look. "Obviously not. Anything else you'd like to check out while you're here? Maybe see my etchings?"

He frowned, looking around the tiny cubicle that made up the bathroom.

"God, I can't believe you've lived here four years, Katie. This place is a dump!"

"It's all I can afford!"

"Past tense. You're moving into my place in five weeks, no make that four."

"Nick ..."

"No, we agreed. And I can't say I'm sorry about this place being torn down. It really is a dump."

"I know that, but I just wish you'd stop pushing me. This agreement we have is a big enough change already. Can you blame me for wanting to take things slow?"

"There's slow and then there's a dead stop, Katie. I just don't want you living in a place like this. Even if it is for only a few more weeks."

"It's been fine for four years."

He shook his head and reached out, his hands on her arms.

"Katie, I know I can come on a little strong, but I worry about you. You've lost a lot of weight in the last two years and I know you're barely eating. Not that you're skinny, but you shouldn't lose any more."

She opened her mouth to argue, but he gently shook her.

"I care about you, okay? I just don't like seeing you suffer like this. You've already been through so much. You don't need to dig your heels in, okay? I'm here to take care of all that."

While Kate appreciated the speech, she still had a stubborn streak a mile wide. Part of her wanted to pull away and tell him it wasn't his place to worry about her but the other part that longed for him to actually love her wanted to give in to those feelings. To, for once, leave her fate in the hands of another. The truth of it all was she was tired; tired of trying to deal with all the stress of the past few years alone, trying to keep a positive outlook when all she saw was negative.

Nick stroked her cheek, pushing her long hair back, then leaned forward and kissed her gently.

"Get dressed," he said softly. "Can't do anything about your hair I guess, but at least put some jeans on."

"Why?" she asked.

"'Cause I don't want guys checking out your hot bod," he said. "Especially in those pants."

She looked down at them with a frown. They weren't anything out of the ordinary. Just black pants which fitted snugly. They were comfortable and that was all she cared about.

"What's wrong with my pants?"

"You don't see it?" Nick asked. He leaned over and ran a hand over her butt cheek. Kate started when he squeezed lightly. "You know, that song about big butts is a total con. I mean, you've got a great butt. Nice and proportional."

She flapped her hand at him and tried to push him away. His nearness was just too much and the hand on her backside was doing strange things to her insides.

"Stop that, Nick!"

He grinned and pulled away. "Sorry," he said, not looking sorry in the slightest.

She rolled her eyes in exasperation and moved past him to grab a pair of jeans from the hanger.

Nick drove them to the local shopping mall, grumbling at the line of cars all waiting to get into a car park. Kate just sat back with a hand over her eyes and listened to him curse and carry on like a petulant child.

"What are you doing that for?" he asked.

"I'm trying to pretend I don't know you," she said.

Nick just grinned at her. "Gotta keep them on their toes," he said.

"Oh right, you yelling and having a tanty is keeping them on their toes. Good to know."

"I'm not having a tanty," he replied. "Things would be fine if they would just hurry up."

"Geez, calm down," Kate said, still not sure why she was even here in the first place. There were times when Nick could be such an idiot.

"Finally!" Nick exclaimed, the rubber tyres squealing on the painted surface as he pulled into a parking spot. He put the car in park and pulled up the handbrake.

Kate got out of the car, noticing Nick had barely given her enough time before he was locking the car and striding toward the entrance. A car horn blared at him as the driver was forced to step on his brake or else hit Nick.

"I'm walking here!" Nick called out, in a passable imitation of Dustin Hoffman.

If Kate thought it was bad enough just getting from the car into the mall, trying to keep up with her friend's long strides, it was worse when he pulled her into a fashion boutique.

"Here, let's try this store," he said, making a beeline for a rack of dresses.

Kate almost had a heart attack at the prices. Each dress cost a minimum of at least half of what she'd make in a week. If she'd been working full-time that was. On the benefit, she barely made half that.

"Nick, I can't …"

He ignored her, grabbing a hanger and holding up the dress to her body, eyeing it critically. It was a strapless dress in an olive green. Not quite drab, but certainly lacking in vibrancy.

"Hmm, no. Colour's wrong." He put it back, then grabbed another dress. Kate could only watch in growing consternation as he thrust dress after dress at her. "Go try those on," he ordered.

She frowned, quickly counting up the hangers. She noticed the dressing room had a limit.

"Nick, I can't try all these on. They only allow three in the dressing rooms."

"So?"

"There are at least eight here."

"They'll make an exception," he told her confidently before striding purposefully up to a sales assistant. "Excuse me, do you work here?"

Kate rolled her eyes. Oh my god, she thought, fighting not to giggle as Nick proceeded to beg and plead for the assistant to make an exception. Then he resorted to flirting and she could tell the girl was fighting the urge not to laugh at his antics.

"Nick, stop it! And don't go batting those baby blues at her either. They have policies for a reason."

He looked at her, thrusting out his bottom lip.

"Party pooper," he said.

The assistant giggled, then turned to her. "I can hold some of those over here if you want to try them on once you're done."

"Thank you," she said, before shooting a glare at Nick. "Grow up!"

She wasn't sure how she could tell Nick that there was no way she could afford to buy any of the dresses she tried on. The first one looked good, the second not so good. She rejected a third of the outfits, only to find Nick had gone hunting for more. There were not only dresses but tops and skirts in an array of colours.

She emerged from the dressing room each time to check out her reflection in the long mirror. Nick stood beside her, clearly making mental notes.

The last outfit he handed her was a pantsuit. The trousers were black while the top was white, with shoestring straps. A black bolero jacket completed the outfit. The contrasting colours gave her pale skin a warmth instead of making her look washed out. Nick seemed to like it, making her spin around slowly.

"Mm, it's missing something," he said. He turned to the sales assistant. "Do you have necklaces? Like, I don't know, a heavy gold chain?"

She nodded and went over to a nearby display, picking up a gold chain. She returned to the dressing room and handed it over.

"It's costume jewellery, but I think it would go well with the outfit."

Nick nodded, standing behind Kate and holding the chain loosely around her neck. "Yeah, looks good." He playfully smacked Kate's backside. "Go get dressed, honey."

Kate shot him a disgruntled look at the way he seemed to be ordering her about, but went back into the cubicle, changing back into her jeans and top. She emerged with the pantsuit, which Nick took off her. There was a pile of clothes on the counter which the sales assistant was busy ringing up.

"Uh …"

Nick shot her a look, handing over his credit card.

"Wear the pantsuit tomorrow night," he said.

"Bossy!" she complained. He grinned at her.

"Oh you love me," he said.

She remained silent, not wanting to give away just how those casually uttered words affected her.

The saleswoman handed over the bags, smiling at them as she did so. Nick turned, a hand laid lightly on her back.

"Give me those," he said.

"I can manage," she replied. There were three bags, each filled with the outfits he'd bought her. They were weighty but not so heavy that she couldn't carry them.

"You need shoes," Nick mused as they left the boutique, placing a hand on her back.

"What's wrong with my shoes?" she asked, sighing in resignation as he guided her to a shoe store. She balked when she read the name above the door. The store, while one of a chain, specialised in high-priced shoes and boots. "Not here," she protested. "They're really expensive."

He looked at her. "You know, my nan used to tell me that you can get away with cheap clothing but you can never skimp on shoes. The higher the price, the better the quality. Plus they usually fit you better. A lot of the cheaper stores cut corners."

"Fine," she said. "You're the boss."

"So sue me if I want my future wife to have the best."

Kate was forced to agree with his grandmother's assessment as she tried on a pair of high-heeled sandals Nick insisted would look good with the pantsuit. They were white with crossover straps at the toes and a double strap to support the ankle. The stiletto heel was a little higher than she was used to but the sandals were very comfortable.

"Those look great," he said. "They really show off your slim ankles."

She felt a little disconcerted as he ran his hand down her calf to cup her ankle. Like before, the implied intimacy in his touch was doing odd things to her body.

The saleswoman, an older lady in her forties, gave them a knowing look as she rang up the sandals. Nick took the bag from her and clasped Kate's hand, leading the way out.

"Last stop," he said, nodding his head toward the jeweller's. "I promise. How about we go grab a bite to eat after this?"

"Okay," she agreed.

A man in a formal suit greeted them in the shop.

"Good afternoon," he said. "How can I help you today?"

"Could we see your engagement rings?" Nick asked.

The man smiled. "Of course." He limped over to a glass counter and unlocked the back. Kate frowned. The shopkeeper appeared to be in his sixties. The knuckles on his hands were red and swollen.

He noticed her looking. "Arthritis," he said.

"Oh, I'm sorry."

He shrugged. "Age catches up with you. Sadly, it means I can no longer keep up with making the jewellery."

Nick nodded. "I saw the closing down sale notice on the door."

"Yes, I'll be retiring once I've sold my stock."

Kate looked around, admiring the pieces. "You made all of this?" she asked.

"Most of it," he said proudly. "My son used to help me. He was going to take over, but ..." She saw grief in his expression. "He passed away a year ago. Cancer."

"I'm sorry to hear that, sir," Nick said.

"I still have my daughter-in-law, and my grandchildren. I've learnt to appreciate the things I do have. I'm sure you understand."

"You must get a lot of couples in," Kate observed as Nick prodded her to begin looking through the selection of rings.

The old man nodded. "You can learn a lot about a young couple by the way they look at each other. I can tell from the two of you that you are going to be very happy together."

Kate didn't want to disillusion the man, listening as he began talking about the couples he'd seen come and go. Most of them, he was happy to say, went on to have very successful marriages.

She saw a ring in white gold with a princess cut diamond. The old man followed her gaze and picked up the ring.

"Yes, that is eighteen carat gold. The diamond is a half-carat. I think it would suit you very well."

She looked up at Nick. "What do you think?"

"Try it on," he replied, taking the ring from the old man's hand. Kate let him put the ring on her finger. It fit perfectly.

Nick smiled softly at her, his thumb stroking the ring. "It's perfect," he said.

The old man beamed at them. He rang up the purchase and wished them happiness for their future.

Kate found herself looking down at the ring on her finger as Nick drove away from the mall. She couldn't help remembering the things the old man had said, wishing that they really were as perfect a fit as the ring.

Chapter Nine

Nick had insisted on using a caterer for the dinner party, saying Kate shouldn't have to do anything that night. He told her she might as well get used to playing hostess as it would be something his social circle would expect of his wife.

She had dressed in the pantsuit and sandals, making sure her make-up wasn't overdone. She wasn't used to applying eyeshadow and eyeliner but had spent the morning at the local department store, getting a make-up demonstration. She'd also had her hair cut at the same hair-stylist Diane had gone to. The woman had also blow-dried it, so her shoulder-length curls were soft, the red locks gleaming with health.

From her fiance's expression, he was more than happy with the effort she had gone to.

"You look beautiful," he said, giving her a quick kiss on the lips. She couldn't help the blush that coloured her cheeks at the simple compliment.

He'd chosen to wear a silk shirt in a sky-blue which brought out the colour in his eyes and black tailored pants which moulded nicely to his butt. Kate couldn't help watching him as he walked, blushing when he caught her staring.

"Why, Miss Delaney, you checking out my butt?" he asked with a mischievous grin.

"I'm pleading the fifth," she returned, laughing.

The doorbell rang just as Nick grabbed her and wrapped his arms around her waist. He sighed dramatically.

"Geez, can't even catch a break long enough to kiss my gorgeous fiancée."

"Oh go answer the door," she ordered. He rolled his eyes.

"Man, get a ring on their finger and they get all bossy," he complained good-naturedly as he walked out to the foyer.

"Miss Delaney?"

She turned and looked at the caterer, who was holding a small tablet. "Yes?"

"I just thought you'd want to check over the schedule. So, drinks and nibbles to be served while the guests arrive and dinner will be at seven-thirty." She continued to go over the schedule with Kate nodding. It felt odd to have someone defer to her but she supposed that was something else she would have to get used to.

Nick came back in, followed by his mother and Perry. He poured them all glasses of champagne.

"So, what's the big news, sweetie?" his mother asked, glancing from her son to Kate.

Kate suppressed the urge to hide her left hand, knowing Diane's sharp eyes would pick up the movement. Nick came to her rescue.

"Later, Mum. Drink your champagne."

The doorbell rang again. Kate figured it was her turn to answer it and put her glass down, offering her fiancé a quick smile before going out. She was surprised yet delighted when she opened the door to see her friend Teri, her eyes widening even as her friend pulled her into a hug.

"What are you doing here?" she asked.

"Nick invited me," her friend replied. She was an attractive woman with wavy blonde hair. She often complained about the thick glasses she had to wear but Kate had always thought they suited her well. "He said you had some big news."

Kate frowned, then remembered Nick had met her friend the Christmas before last when she'd gone with her friend to a party at Nick's company. He'd told her to invite someone and she hadn't been able to think of anyone else.

The next surprise was a less pleasant one. It was her former boss, Joy, who was accompanying a man Kate had met at another of Nick's company functions. From the way the woman was wrapped around the man, it looked like she was his date. He seemed less than happy about it. The older woman scowled at her.

"What are you doing here?" she asked rudely.

Kate didn't answer her, showing her best friend into the main room. As she poured glasses of champagne for the new arrivals, she quickly noticed Joy making a beeline for Nick. Her fiancé scowled at her former boss. He was clearly not happy to see her. The woman didn't seem to notice, ignoring her date to cosy up to Nick.

Her fiancé seemed relieved when more guests announced their arrival, quickly going out to the foyer. He glanced at her on the way and gave her a little smile.

Kate tried to ignore her ex-boss and chose to chat to her friend. Clearly piqued with the way Nick had ignored her, Joy cut in.

"So, what are you doing with yourself these days?" she asked, speaking loud enough for all those gathered to hear. She eyed the outfit Kate was wearing. "Looks like you've done all right for yourself. That's certainly no cheap knock-off you're wearing," she added pointedly.

She had always been highly critical of Kate's clothing when she had worked at the gallery, putting Kate down for wearing clothes she claimed she 'wouldn't be caught dead in'.

"Got yourself a sugar daddy?" The woman laughed harshly.

"If she did, it's none of your business," Teri told her coolly, making it clear she disliked the older woman and didn't appreciate the interruption in their conversation.

"Just taking an interest," Joy returned.

"No, you're sticking your nose in where it's not wanted," Kate replied. "I don't work for you anymore, so how about you keep your insinuations to yourself?"

The older woman looked insulted, bristling visibly.

"Well! I never!" She turned to Nick who had come back into the room. "Are you going to stand there and let her speak to me like that?"

"It's no more than what you deserve," he told her. "Maybe Kate was never allowed to speak her mind and tell you exactly what she thought of you the whole time she was working for you, but as my future wife, she has every right to tell you that you are a grade-A bitch and not even a tenth of the woman she is."

Joy stared at him, her eyes wide and her face pale with shock. "What did you just say?"

Nick glanced at Kate, giving her a sheepish look. "Sorry, honey," he said. "I didn't mean to announce it that way."

"It's all right," she replied, moving to his side and giving him a quick kiss. He wrapped an arm around her waist and turned to their guests.

"So, uh, for those who didn't hear that, Kate and I are getting married."

"Well, it's about bloody time!" Perry called out, making the others laugh.

"Hear hear," Diane added as guests began to give their congratulations.

Perry grabbed a utensil and began tapping on his glass. "A toast," he announced. "To the happy couple, who have finally woken up to what the rest of us have known for some time."

Nick grinned and kissed her before raising his glass to his lips. Before he could drink, someone else proposed a toast.

"To Kate, who is clearly the only woman capable of keeping Nick in line."

"I'll drink to that," another guest called out, eliciting much laughter from the others.

Kate looked up at Nick. He was smiling, his eyes sparkling. She swallowed the lump in her throat. She loved seeing him so happy but couldn't help waiting for the bubble to burst. As she looked around at the guests, she noticed the look on Joy's face. The woman was glaring daggers at her.

She managed to get away a short while later and went out to the courtyard for a little bit of air. As she sat in one of the wicker chairs she heard footsteps and looked around. Diane came to sit in the chair next to her.

"A little hot in there," she said, waving a hand in front of her face as if to demonstrate how warm it was. Kate appreciated the little white lie. "How are you doing sweetie?"

"I'm fine," she assured her future mother-in-law.

"You can't fool me. It can be a little overwhelming, can't it?" she said.

"It's all happened rather fast, to be honest."

"Well, if you want my two cents', I'm happy you persuaded Nicky to wait until after Christmas to have the wedding. Goodness knows it's a stressful time of the year during the holidays." She looked at Diane. Nick had already told the guests when they were getting married but not how the date had been chosen. Kate guessed he'd given his mother a few more details.

"You don't think it's too long?"

"No," the other woman laughed. "Goodness no. I know my son and he can be so impatient sometimes. I'm glad he chose you, sweetie. You have a way of reining in his more impulsive nature."

"Oh, I don't know about that. He still manages to get himself in trouble on occasion."

Diane grinned at her. "Of that I have no doubt. I remember when he was a teenager and he was so keen on becoming a race car driver. There was no way I was going to let him do so and I knew his father would refuse him. He was more than a little upset with me for a while after that." She put a hand on Kate's knee. "Not that he would do that to you, sweetheart. He loves you too much."

Kate didn't comment, figuring it was better for Diane to remain under the illusion that they were getting married for love.

"For what it's worth, darling, I think you and Nicky are perfect for each other and I know you'll have a wonderful life together. Don't worry about people like Joy. She had no right to treat you the way she did and I'm glad you put her in her place." She stood up, smiling at Nick, who had come out. "By the way," she added, "you look lovely tonight. Doesn't she darling?"

"Yeah Mum, she does," he said, watching as his mother stepped back inside. He sat down in his mother's place. "Everything okay?" he asked.

"Yeah," she replied. "It just got a bit … you know."

He took her hand and rubbed it gently. "I know. But I think you handled yourself rather well in there, especially with Joy. She left, by the way. I made it clear she hadn't been invited and she wasn't welcome."

"I'm sorry if what I said came off sounding rude."

He shook his head. "No, if anyone was rude, she was. You said exactly the right thing without getting nasty about it. Joy's always been a piece of work. I mean, I know it put you in a bad position when you left, but I'm glad you're out of that gallery."

"Me too," she agreed, happy to say that it was true. She wouldn't have been able to stomach the woman's vitriol much longer.

He leaned over and kissed her. "Come on. They're about to serve dinner and I don't know about you, but I'm starving."

She let him pull her up and take her hand as they walked back inside.

Chapter Ten

"Well, these look nice."

Kate paused from looking through the rack of wedding dresses to turn to her friend. Teri had been searching through another rack of gowns, pulling out a couple. One of them had either sequins or beads decorating the bodice. She couldn't quite see which.

"I don't ... know," she said uncertainly.

Diane took the beaded dress from Teri and held it up. "Why don't you try it on, sweetie? You can never tell just by holding it up against you."

She was right, but then Nick's mother always was. Diane had been the one to suggest they go shopping for a wedding dress, telling her that it was never too early to do so, despite the date being over two months away. As her future mother-in-law reminded her, she would probably have to have alterations done and the dress would need to be laundered before the ceremony anyway.

The older woman had driven them to a boutique on the main street of a small town about twenty minutes' drive from the city. She knew the owner, an older woman who designed and made wedding dresses.

While they were still more than Kate could afford, they weren't as expensive as other stores.

She'd already looked at a few of the dresses but had been reluctant to try them on. She still didn't even know what kind of ceremony Nick had planned. He had insisted on taking care of all those details himself.

Her fiancé had thrown himself into organising the wedding with an enthusiasm she had never seen before. Nick seemed to relish the opportunity. Now that the contract to buy the smaller company had been signed and sealed, he wasn't as stressed and had more energy to devote to other things.

Kate still felt like the event was going to be more like a coronation than an actual wedding but she wasn't about to complain. Her future husband seemed to be bent on showing her that they could be happy together and she had to admit that she felt happier than she had been in years.

He was still insisting she move in with him. She had a couple of weeks left at the flat and she wasn't going to do anything to give the landlord reason to deny her bond refund.

A nudge from Teri reminded her where they were and she took the dress from Diane, going to the dressing room to change out of her outfit. She examined the cream-coloured dress closely. It was strapless with beadwork laid out in a pretty design which covered the bodice and ran down the long skirt. The back of the bodice was held together with hooks and eyes.

The owner called out cheerily.

"Need any help dear?"

She bit her lip. "Um, yes, if you don't mind helping me do up the back?"

The woman entered the dressing room. Kate held the dress up. It was slightly too big for her.

"Don't worry about the size, dear," the lady said. She was a kind-looking woman in her late fifties. Kate watched in the mirror as she began doing up the back. "I can alter this to fit you. Now, how about we go and show … your mother, is she?"

"Mother-in-law," Kate corrected with a smile. Diane might be Nick's mother but she felt in the past few weeks she had grown closer than ever to the older woman. She followed the owner out, standing on a small circular platform so the fitting could be checked. Diane and Teri looked at her, both smiling.

"That's the one," Diane said. "It looks beautiful on you, darling."

"It really does," Teri echoed.

"Your parents would have been so proud to see you on your wedding day," Diane told her.

Kate nodded. Her parents would never have been able to afford a dress like this, but it didn't matter. She had tears in her eyes as she gazed at her reflection in the long mirror. With her hair up, showing her long, graceful neck, it would be perfect.

"This is really happening, isn't it?" she breathed.

Teri grinned. "Yeah, it is."

"Of course, we have to find you a dress too," she told her friend. Teri's eyes widened. The other woman had never been one for what she called girly clothing.

"A dress?"

"Well, it's kind of expected for the maid of honour to wear a dress," Kate replied, laughing at her friend's expression.

"Oh my god, you really …"

"Did you think I would ask anyone else?" Kate reached out and hugged her friend.

Before they could look for a dress for her friend, she still had to stand still so the shop owner could get all the measurements she required to fit the dress.

"You could stand to put on a little weight," the woman replied. "You're far too skinny."

"That's what I've been telling her," Diane told her friend.

"Oh don't worry. Nick's taking care of that as well," Kate returned, laughing.

At her fiance's insistence, she had lunch with him every second day and dinner every night at his house. They usually took turns cooking but they would cook together on weekends if they hadn't spent the day out. Nick had decided he liked experimenting with different dishes and was always looking up recipes he thought they should try.

With the evenings getting lighter, they often went out for walks together to the lagoon or through the botanical gardens. It gave Nick a chance to unwind from work. They would also often talk about things they had seen or heard during the day.

Nick had also insisted on taking care of her bills, despite his continued attempts to persuade her to move in with him. He'd also heard from the lawyer handling the investigation into the finance company. While it would take some time for the case to be heard, the lawyer hadn't been optimistic about Kate's chances of recovering the money they had fraudulently taken from her. The news hadn't made her fiancé happy as he told her he felt she deserved to get all the money she had paid back, but Kate was philosophical about it. She had heard dozens of stories of victims of various scams who had lost thousands of dollars and she considered herself reasonably lucky. There had been an article published in the newspaper about the company which included an interview with another victim who had lost their home.

Kate had given a lot of thought to her future and had made a decision. When she sat down to dinner that night with Nick, she broached the subject.

"I've been doing a lot of thinking," she said.

"About what, honey?" he asked, picking up her plate and serving her a helping of salad.

"About the future. What I want to do with my life."

He smiled at her. "I'm listening."

"Well, a few weeks ago I was talking with your mum and she asked me what I wanted to do, as a career, I mean. So, anyway, I went to the museum and I had a meeting with the curator. I can work there on a voluntary basis, part-time. Then when uni starts up again, I'm going to enrol for a diploma in museum studies. I'm not sure what my job prospects will be at the end of it, but Mr Cameron said I might be able to get paid work once I finished the diploma. What do you think?"

He took little time to consider the question, grinning at her.

"I think that's great, honey. How much do you think you'll need for tuition costs?"

"I have to find out from the university, but I guess I could always get a student loan."

He shook his head. "Nope. What you said the other day about marriage being a partnership goes both ways. If this is something you want, then I can cover the costs. And don't argue," he said, pointing his fork at her.

She mock-saluted him. "Yes, boss."

He munched on some of his salad, then sipped his wine.

"So how did the shopping trip go?"

"Great," she said. "We found a dress."

"Am I allowed to see this dress?"

"Nope."

He pouted. "Why not?"

"You know very well why not, Nick Sloane, so don't pull the puppy dog trick with me. Anyway, the dress has to be altered. Although," she added, groaning and pushing her chair away from the table, "with what you've been feeding me lately, I'm starting to think the dress won't fit me in two months anyway."

"Not a chance," he replied.

After they'd cleaned the kitchen together, they went out for their usual nightly walk.

"So when are you going to move in?" he asked.

"When my tenancy is up," she told him. "We've been over this. I'm not giving the landlord the excuse to withhold my bond."

"Okay, fine," he said.

They walked along the edge of the lagoon. There were a few cars parked along the roadside. A couple of families had bought some takeaways and were eating them at the picnic tables, watching the ducks. A toddler was running around chasing the animals. Nick stopped walking for a moment, watching the little boy.

"Shouldn't they be keeping an eye on him?" he asked.

"Who?"

"Whoever his parents are." None of the adults seated at the tables appeared to care what the toddler was up to. "You know, when we have kids, there's no way I'm going to just turn my back on them like that."

They continued walking.

"Little reality check, Nick. You can't watch kids twenty-four seven. I mean, okay, you've got a point. Especially when there's a body of water nearby. But kids do tend to wander off. It's the parents who leave their children in stores and expect the staff to babysit that's the problem. Like they don't take responsibility for them."

"Sounds like you're speaking from experience."

She nodded. She had worked in a store while she was studying for her degree and some children, the oldest no more than age seven, had been left in the store. Another staff member had overheard the mother telling them to stay put while she went shopping elsewhere in the mall. The store had got busy and none of the staff could watch the children so when they'd wandered off, no one knew where they were. The mother had returned and threatened to call the police because the staff hadn't bothered to watch the children. Finally, mall security had been called. Kate learnt later that the children had been found in another store. Mall management had contacted the local child welfare office and reported the mother for neglect.

Nick was incensed when she told him the story. "People like that should be tested for stupidity. I mean, there are creches at some of the malls now. Besides, if you don't want your kids around while you're shopping, hire a babysitter."

"Yeah," she agreed. While her parents hadn't been as bad, they had often let her do whatever she wanted as a teenager. She had been caught shoplifting when she was twelve, although she'd only done it on a dare. Her mother had been called but she hadn't even bothered to punish her. The humiliation and embarrassment of being caught by security had been enough of a deterrent that Kate never did it again.

Nick laughed when she told him the story. "I can't imagine you ever doing anything like shoplifting."

"Once was enough, believe me."

"Your parents really didn't care?"

She shook her head. "Nope. I mean, I don't want to say they were bad parents or anything. They just didn't worry about little things like that. I guess I was pretty independent from a young age."

"Mum would have whacked my butt if I did anything like that or talked back to her. I once mouthed off to her when I was about sixteen. I think it was around the same time as I started talking about wanting to be a race car driver. She told me I wasn't too old for her to take me over her knee."

Kate chuckled. "Yeah, I can just see that. Your mum can be seriously scary when she wants to be."

"Wait until we have kids. She's going to spoil them rotten."

"Well, that's what grandmothers are for." She looked up at him. "Have you told your dad?"

He shook his head. "No. My dad's not part of my life, so I'd rather not say anything. He's not invited to the wedding anyway."

"Speaking of which, are you ever going to tell me what you have planned?"

"What's there to tell? Your job is just to show up on the day and promise to love, honour and obey."

"Oh, like fun I'm going to promise to obey." He laughed, making it clear he was teasing her. She glared at him. "You are a rotten tease, Nick Sloane."

He let go of her hand and turned, cocking an eyebrow at her. "What are you gonna do about it, Miss Delaney?" His grin was wicked.

"Ooh, you are so gonna get it!"

He laughed harder. "You'd have to catch me first." With that he took off running. Kate chased after him, threatening all manner of punishments if she caught him.

He caught her instead, lifting her up and kissing her soundly. They walked back to the house, their arms wrapped around each other.

Nick kept a firm grasp on her hand as they entered the house, pulling her toward the stairs. "Stay," he said.

"I … I don't have my clothes," she objected.

"I'll lend you my t-shirt."

"Nick …"

"I'm just talking about sleeping. I know you want to wait until we get married and I'm fine with that. I just want to hold you. Is that okay?"

She lay with her back to him, his arm around her waist as he spooned against her, holding her close. She knew from the quiet snores that he was deeply asleep but it somehow eluded her. She just couldn't stop thinking about the situation. How was she going to manage wanting to be with someone who couldn't or wouldn't return her love?

Chapter Eleven

The next two months passed all too quickly for Kate. She had moved all her meagre possessions into the house once her tenancy was up. She had no idea what her ex-landlord was going to do with the furniture but it wasn't her problem.

Nick had been surprised at how little she actually owned. She had to remind him that she had lost everything in the fire that had killed her parents and just hadn't had the money to replace anything. She had boarded with family friends for a couple of years before moving into a shared flat, which was how she had got to know Luke. Since each place she'd moved into had been fully furnished, she hadn't worried about getting any of her own.

She was still reticent about sleeping with her soon-to-be husband. Despite his continued insistence that this was going to be a 'real' marriage, with all that went with it, she didn't know how to avoid giving away her feelings for him. It had made for more than a few sleepless nights, lying next to him, wanting him and feeling him so close to her.

The night before the wedding, Diane had arranged it that she and Teri would have a room at a hotel in town.

She also insisted on inviting a few ladies for drinks in the hotel bar. Kate was too nervous, feeling like her stomach was tied up in knots, to even think about drinking.

"Sweetheart, trust me. A few of these drinks in you and you'll sleep like a baby. You want to be bright-eyed and bushy-tailed for the ceremony tomorrow."

"Ugh, I think I want to throw up," Kate moaned.

"Now don't talk like that. Come on. At least have a few sips of this." The older woman thrust a cocktail glass in front of her. It was filled with a red liquid.

"What is it?"

"A margarita. Don't tell me you've never had one before."

"Um, no." She picked up the glass and tasted the drink. It was all right. Not quite sweet, with a little edge to it. "What's in a margarita?" she asked.

"Tequila, triple sec and usually lime or lemon but this one has strawberry." Diane put a hand on her shoulder. "Darling, you're too tense."

"I just … I'm nervous. About tomorrow."

"Well, that's understandable, sweetie. You're getting married! Believe me, I was a mess the night before my wedding."

And we all know how that turned out, Kate thought. From the look on Diane's face, she wondered if she'd said that out loud. When the older woman spoke again, it assured her that she hadn't.

"Oh, I know what you're thinking. Nick's father walked away from our marriage, but I loved him. In many ways I still do."

"Why did he leave?" she asked, remembering her initial thoughts that maybe Nick's father had been abusive, but Diane shook her head in denial, assuring Kate there hadn't been anything of the sort.

"Gavin just wasn't cut out to be a husband and father, I suppose. He wasn't happy when I became pregnant with Nick, but you know, Nicky's the best thing that ever happened to me." She smiled warmly at Kate. "I'm sure he's the best thing that ever happened to you too."

She didn't know what to say to that. The conversation somehow turned to children.

"Nick keeps talking about having a family."

"Well, Nicky adores kids," Diane said. "He gets that from me. Did you know he volunteers as a big brother?"

She nodded, sipping her drink. She was still not sure of the taste but it did seem to be relaxing her a little.

"He loves it. He's always talking about how he likes to teach the kids things that their parents should have done. He keeps saying he'll never be like that."

The older woman looked thoughtful. "I suppose in some ways I spoiled him, but then I was trying to make up for his father rarely being there."

"He doesn't blame you, you know. You did the best you could."

"Thank you, darling. You're a treasure and I hope my son realises that."

Kate bit her lip, wishing she knew exactly what Nick was thinking. Teri nudged her.

"So where is your future husband?"

She shrugged. "I don't know. He did mention something about having a few drinks with the boys." She frowned. "I hope they're not planning on playing any tricks on him. I used to know this guy who told me that when a friend of his was getting married, they decided to chain him up to a lamp post and put a sign around his neck."

"It could have been worse," Diane commented. "At least they didn't tar and feather him."

"Guys do that?" Teri asked, incredulous.

"Well, I don't know about tar. Perhaps they use black paint instead. I'm sure it's quite a comical sight."

"Perry better not be thinking about doing the same thing to Nick," Kate returned with a growl of annoyance. "Or I will have words."

"Ooh, sounds like somebody's going to be in trouble if he does."

There was a murmur in the bar. "Speak of the devil!" Diane said in a low voice.

Kate looked up. Nick had walked in and was making a beeline for her.

"Nicholas Sloane, what do you think you're doing?" his mother asked.

"Butt out, Mother, I want to talk to my gorgeous fiancée."

Perry was trailing behind, trying to look as if he'd had nothing to do with it, but Kate could see Nick was more than a little tipsy. He grabbed her hand and pulled her up from the stool.

"Katie …"

"Nick, I don't know what you think you're doing, but you're drunk."

"I don't care. I just wanted to tell you … you're so beautiful Katie. I can't believe in less than twenty-four hours you'll be mine."

He was definitely marching to the beat of his own drum, she thought as he swept her up and tried to get her to dance with him. She couldn't help but laugh at his antics, even as she worried he was going to be hung over the next day.

She glared at Perry. "If he's hungover tomorrow, you are sooo dead!"

"I'll consider that a warning," the other man said, grabbing Nick's arm. "Come on, lover boy. I think it's time we got you home to bed before your fiancée makes good on her threat."

She couldn't tell what they were talking about as Perry led Nick away but her fiancé was gesturing emphatically. Perry shot her an apologetic look as they left the hotel.

"Hmm, it is getting late," Diane said, glancing at the clock on her phone. "You need your beauty sleep."

Kate thought she would be too wound up to sleep but either the margarita had relaxed her just enough or Diane had slipped something in with the alcohol. She woke the next morning feeling completely refreshed, although the butterflies returned with a vengeance as soon as she looked at the clock and realised she had a little over four hours to get ready for the ceremony.

Diane came to her rescue once again, giving her a glass of champagne and orange juice.

"It's called a mimosa," she said, handing glasses to both Kate and Teri. "I'm not planning on getting you drunk but I don't want you getting nervous either."

The phone rang and she glanced at the screen before picking up the call. "Good morning darling. How are you feeling this morning?" There was a long pause. Kate assumed Nick was answering his mother's query. Diane looked at her. "She's right here," she said, handing Kate the phone.

"Hi honey," Nick said. "How are you feeling?"

"A bit nervous, actually," she admitted.

"I know. Me too. It'll be okay. Just try to relax and visualise walking down that aisle. I'll be waiting at the end for you."

"Nick …"

"Yeah, Katie."

"I …" She couldn't say it. As much as she wanted to tell him she loved him, she didn't want to risk it. She couldn't say it and know that he wouldn't say it back. "I'll see you soon, okay?"

Teri glanced at the clock. "We gotta move it," she said. "We're due at the hairdressers in twenty minutes."

"Sounds like you need to get going," Nick commented. "See you later honey."

The hairdresser was the same one who had done Kate's hair for the engagement party. Kate tried not to squirm in the chair as the woman brushed and teased the curls. She had chosen to keep her natural curl rather than straightening her hair. The sides were neatly pinned with the long locks allowed to flow down her back. She had earlier thought she should have put it all up but the hairdresser had convinced her this would work better since she wasn't wearing a veil.

"You have such lovely red hair," Diane remarked. "I went to school with this girl - she was a proper carrot top. Poor thing was teased mercilessly about being ginger."

Kate had once had the same problem until she had stood up to the bullies. Her grandfather had told her that his father had once had the same problem in his school days in Ireland. Freddy Delaney had dealt with it the way all men in his generation had dealt with it. With his fists. That option hadn't been available to Kate, but she was still from good Irish stock and she had let the bullies know in no uncertain terms that she didn't have to take their nonsense.

Nick seemed to love the colour of her hair. He couldn't get enough of touching it, wondering aloud if it was possible to recreate such a colour. '

"Ooh look, there she goes, daydreaming about her handsome husband-to-be," Teri teased. Kate glanced at her friend in the mirror, feeling her cheeks burning.

"Was not," she said.

"Yeah, sure you weren't," the blonde replied. The hairdresser's sister was working on the other woman's hair. Both women ran the salon together.

The woman working on Kate pulled the cape off.

"All done," she said. About a minute later her sister announced she was done with Teri's hair. Kate's maid of honour had opted for a French knot, sweeping her shoulder-length hair back into a jewelled clip. The style was elegant without looking too elaborate.

"All right, ladies. We have an hour to get make-up done and get ready before we have to leave for the ceremony." Diane smiled at the two sisters. "Once again, Beth and Marjorie, you have outdone yourselves."

Marjorie smiled back. "Anything for you and your beautiful daughter-in-law, Mrs Sloane." She leaned forward and kissed Kate's cheek. "We wish you all the best for your future."

"Thank you," Kate replied, letting herself be swept out of the salon.

Her nerves returned with a vengeance once her make-up was done. She trembled as she slipped her dress on, wondering why she felt so anxious. Teri helped her do up the hooks and eyes in the back.

"Just remember, Nick loves you," she said.

Kate nodded, not wanting to tell her friend the truth. As far as anyone knew, they were madly, passionately in love. Why disillusion them? she thought.

Diane looked them both over. Teri had chosen a chiffon sun-dress in a creamy colour which went well with her blonde hair. The back of the dress was plain and the front had a floral pattern in gold. It was simple but beautiful, suiting her slender frame.

"You both look lovely," the older woman said. She herself had decided to wear a skirt and jacket in a pastel blue with a simple white silk top underneath the jacket.

Kate was surprised when she saw the car waiting for them outside the hotel, a uniformed chauffeur standing by the back door, ready to usher them inside. Nick had hired a white stretch limousine, a vehicle which was a rare sight in the city. The hire of the car with chauffeur, must have cost Nick a fortune, she decided.

She couldn't help but grin at the stares from people as they passed by. It sounded a little silly, but she felt a little bit like royalty sitting in the back of the limousine while Diane and Teri opposite her, their backs facing the driver.

"I feel like a movie star," Teri said with a grin.

"That's probably what people are thinking when they see the car," Kate replied.

"When my son decides to do something, he doesn't do it by halves," Diane commented.

Kate knew Nick was trying to make her feel special. Still, she wouldn't have cared if they'd used a horse and cart. The only thing she needed to feel that way was marrying the man she loved and knowing he loved her.

More surprises were in store when the limousine came to a stop. Kate had mentioned some weeks earlier that she had always thought getting married in a beautiful setting like the rose garden was in some ways better than being married in a church. Since neither she nor Nick was particularly religious, she had wondered if he had chosen to go the traditional route.

The rose gardens were part of a large public green space. There were walkways through bush as well as aviaries housing various birds and playgrounds for young children to play on. Every summer the local community groups put on a few events including a fair and a teddy bears' picnic for the children. Kate had once told Nick it had been one of her favourite places to go as a child and in many ways it still was.

She walked down the path behind Teri, refusing to let her nerves get the better of her. She kept her head up and looked straight ahead at the man she loved. His eyes never left her face, watching her slowly approach. Still, she was relieved when she finally reached his side and let him take her arm.

He winked at her before they both turned to face the celebrant. She couldn't help stealing glances at him even as the ceremony began. He looked so handsome in his dark grey suit. He also wore a gold tie which matched the gold in Teri's dress. His hair, usually messy, had been cut and styled so there wasn't a hair out of place. Perry stood beside him in the same colour suit.

Nick caught her glance and squeezed her hand, nudging her to pay attention to the celebrant.

"Family and friends, we are gathered here to witness the joining of Nicholas and Katherine in marriage."

Chapter Twelve

Just as he had with the wedding ceremony, Nick had kept Kate in the dark about where he had planned their honeymoon. She had asked him a couple of times but he had refused to tell her anything. All she knew was that they would have to fly to Auckland and from there would fly to their mystery destination.

The only thing Kate had had to do was get a passport. Nick had organised everything else, down to the smallest detail.

She looked at her new husband as they left the domestic terminal in Auckland.

"So are you going to tell me where we're going?"

"Nope," he replied, shaking his head.

"Not even a hint?"

"Not even a hint," he said, his mouth twitching. "Stop it."

"Stop what?"

"You know what they say about curiosity, don't you?"

She huffed at him. "You're mean!" She pouted.

He pulled her close and kissed her. "So I'm mean, am I? Good to know."

"Nicholas …" she began, narrowing her eyes at him, but he growled back at her.

"Don't even think it, Mrs Sloane. Only my mother ever gets away with calling me Nicholas."

Kate felt a tiny shiver up her spine. He'd called her 'Mrs Sloane'. It felt almost surreal. Here they were, married.

Nick led her to a chair and handed her the Kindle he'd bought her once they'd checked in and got through the security area. He'd had the device loaded up with some of her favourite books.

"Might as well settle in. Our flight's not boarding until ten." Nick glanced at the clock above the monitors which showed the flights scheduled that evening. "It's only a few minutes after eight."

"I'm going to find out you know," Kate told him smugly. "I'll just study the schedule."

"Yeah, good luck. Considering we have a short layover first."

"Where?" she asked.

He smirked. "Yeah, nice try."

"Okay, how about twenty questions. I'll ask a question and you tell me if I'm getting warmer."

"Are you trying to trick me, Katie?"

She raised her eyebrows and tried to look innocent. "Who? Me?"

"Yes, you." He smirked in amusement. "All right. Fine. We'll play it your way. You ask me questions, but I'll only answer yes or no. So, what's your first question?"

Kate studied the schedules. She figured if the plane was boarding around ten pm, it would be at least half an hour to forty-five minutes before take-off. She checked the list for flights departing around that time.

"Okay, first question. Is the destination a primarily English-speaking country?"

"No," he replied. "Second question?"

"Is the layover in a primarily English-speaking country?"

"No."

Well, that left out Sydney and Melbourne, she thought, seeing both those flights were departing around the same time. There were still five other destinations which might fit, each flight departing within the space of fifteen minutes. She sat back, glaring at the monitor. This was going to be harder than she thought.

"Hmm, okay, does the place we're going to accept the Euro or the American dollar?"

"That's two questions. And the answer is no for both. Four down, sixteen to go."

She scowled at him. "I hate you."

"Oh, charming. Married six, no make that seven hours," he said, looking at his watch, "and my wife hates me already."

She stuck out her lower lip in an exaggerated pout. "You are so mean!" she repeated.

"Watch that lip or you'll trip over it."

She was forced to laugh. "That's so stupid! That sounds like something my Grandad used to say."

"Still funny though," Nick replied. He draped an arm over her shoulders. "Enough with the questions already, okay? I wanted this to be a surprise; one I think you'll really like. But we have a long flight ahead of us. I just want you to sit back and enjoy it."

She relented at his expression. "Okay," she agreed.

She picked up her Kindle reader and switched it on, accessing one of her favourite books from the library. It was a romantic drama published years before Kate was born, but she had borrowed a copy from the city library as a teenager and had loved it ever since. The main character had been framed for a crime she didn't commit and after being sent to prison, was forced to become a thief, only to fall for a fellow thief.

Nick read over her shoulder.

"Sidney Sheldon? Wasn't he the guy who wrote that tv series about a genie?"

"*I Dream of Jeannie*. He was also a best-selling novelist."

"Whatever floats your boat, babe." She glanced at him. He was scratching just under his nose. "You know, Barbara Eden was hot in her day."

"That is such a typical male thing to say."

"Ahh, come on, girls, sorry, women do it too. I've seen you perving those guys on that show."

"Do not," she replied. "Anyway, that's a little vague. Which show are you talking about?"

"You mean there's more than one?" he asked. Kate wrinkled her nose at him.

"That one about the guys who chase monsters. And you do too," he added.

"This is such a weird conversation to be having with, you know, my husband, of all people."

He grinned. "Okay, I'll make you a deal, Mrs Sloane. I'll let you keep on perving those guys if you let me have my fun. Besides, there's only one woman I will ever want or need in my life and that's you."

She wrinkled her nose at him. "Flattery will get you nowhere," she replied in a singsong voice.

He smirked back at her. "Just you wait until I get you alone in our villa at the resort," he returned.

Kate felt an odd sensation at his words, almost like they'd gone down a sudden steep drop. Her mouth felt strangely dry at the thought of what was going to be happening once they were alone.

It wasn't that she hadn't slept with other men but the experience had been nothing spectacular. She had never asked Nick how much experience he had but guessed it was a lot more than hers.

She tried to turn her attention back to reading but the issue bothered her more than she wanted to admit. For all that this was still, in her mind, a marriage of convenience, Nick was adamant that it would be a real marriage with all that that entailed. To her the fact that they had slept in the same bed together for two months was irrelevant. Her husband had respected her enough not to push the issue of sex between them, probably thinking she wanted to wait until they got married.

Of course, now that they were actually married, there was no reason for her to refuse him. That scared her.

An announcement came over the loudspeaker but Kate was too absorbed in her thoughts to pay any attention. It wasn't until Nick nudged her that she understood.

"That's us," he said.

They held hands as they walked, cabin baggage in hand, to the gate where the plane was waiting for them. A check-in attendant was waiting beside the exit checking boarding passes. She smiled in greeting and wished them a good flight.

A few minutes later they were settled in the cabin. Kate was not surprised to discover that Nick had paid for seats in business class instead of economy. The seats were more comfortable and had extra leg room, or so she'd been told. Since she had never flown internationally before, she didn't really know enough to judge which was better.

The flight attendants bustled about as the passengers filed in and settled in their seats. It took a little while before everyone was aboard and the staff began their pre-flight checks. Kate felt nervous as she watched the attendant go through the safety instructions.

Nick smiled reassuringly at her. "You okay?"

"Just a little nervous," she said.

"Hey, this is no different than flying domestic."

"It's not that," she said. "I mean, yeah, it is that a little. It's just … well, we're flying to some foreign country and I don't know what I'm supposed to do, or …"

He put a hand on hers, squeezing gently. "Honey, relax. It'll be fine. Where we're going, they have tourists all the time. Besides, it's our honeymoon. It's not like they'll be expecting us to go to any social things. I imagine they'll be thinking we'll be holed up in our villa the whole two weeks."

"Two weeks?" she asked, aware of a squeak in her voice. She couldn't stay in a villa for two whole weeks. What would people think? What if he wanted to stay in bed the whole time?

Nick continued to reassure her as the plane taxied out to the runway. She heard the engine noise increase in volume as the pilot waited for his clearance, then turned onto the runway itself. She watched the terminal building whizzing by as the plane picked up speed and suddenly they were in the air, climbing up to several thousand feet. She pressed her head against the backrest, trying to calm the butterflies in her stomach.

She tried a few deep breaths to calm down. Nick seemed to think she was just nervous from the flight and the last thing she wanted to tell him was that the actual cause of her nerves was the thought of them having sex. Especially over the entire length of their honeymoon.

There was movement in the cabin and she looked up to see the flight attendants moving about, offering the passengers drinks.

"Sir? Ma'am? Would you like something to drink?"

"Some wine would be nice," Nick said. He reached over and squeezed Kate's hand. "We just got married."

The attendant smiled. "Well, congratulations. I'm afraid I can't offer champagne, but we do have some sparkling white wine. It's local, from a Marlborough vineyard."

"That sounds great," he said, beaming at her. "Thank you."

The wine was duly poured. Kate sipped hers, letting the alcohol relax her. The attendants brought around snacks for those who were still awake but it wasn't long before the combination of the excitement of the day and the wine made her sleepy. Nick draped a blanket over her and kissed her cheek as he helped her settle.

"Aren't you sleepy?" she asked.

"Nah. I'm gonna watch a movie or something. Go to sleep honey."

Despite the strangeness of their surroundings, Kate did find herself dozing off. She briefly woke a few times and noticed her husband had dozed off and pulled half the blanket so they were sharing. The lights in the cabin had been dimmed, but not so much that people couldn't see if they needed to go to the bathroom.

In the early hours of the morning, she found herself unable to get back to sleep. She turned and gazed at her husband's face as he slept. Nick seemed to look younger, the lines which had started to form around his eyes and mouth almost smooth. She wanted to reach over and gently trace the contours of his face, kiss his lips, whisper soft words of love to him. Yet she couldn't seem to work up the courage to do so.

God, she loved him.

I can do this, she thought. Maybe he didn't feel the same way about her that she felt about him, but he was still here with her. They were married. Other marriages had survived on a lot less.

His eyes opened and he gazed at her sleepily.

"Hi," she said shyly.

"Hi, yourself. What are you doing?"

"Just looking. I'm allowed, aren't I?"

He smiled softly. "Oh yeah, that's definitely allowed." He raised his arm from under the blanket to glance at his watch. "It's early. Go back to sleep."

"I'm not that tired anymore," she said.

"Want to watch a movie?"

"Okay." Together they looked through the movie selection and found something that seemed interesting. Nick wrapped his arm around her shoulders and held her close as they watched the movie.

Shortly after breakfast was served, the announcement came that they were an hour away from landing in Dubai. She still wasn't sure exactly where their final destination was but she had decided it didn't matter. Nick wouldn't take her on holiday to a place he knew she wouldn't like.

The connecting flight wasn't nearly as long as their first one but by the time they did reach the island of Mauritius they were both feeling jet-lagged and Kate was more than a little grumpy. They'd been flying for most of the last twenty-four hours. What felt like late at night for her was mid-afternoon local time by the time they left the airport. Her husband seemed to understand completely.

"Never mind honey. The resort's not far away. We'll soon be settled into our villa."

She yawned. "I could do with a nana nap," she said.

He shook his head. "Bad idea, sweetie. They tell you not to go to sleep too early when you're jet-lagged. Especially when you're in a completely different time zone."

She wasn't sure she could last until bedtime, continuing to yawn as the resort's private shuttle took them and the other passengers to check in. She was still yawning as they were escorted to the villa where they would stay for the next two weeks.

As soon as they unpacked, Kate wanted to relax with a glass of cool juice. The temperature outside was fairly hot and she was already sweating. The resort manager had also told them January was usually the wettest month and the humidity was fairly high.

The villa had a terrace where she could sit and enjoy the scenery. The roof of the villa extended out so there was shade. She knew from painful experience how quickly she burned in the sun and had made sure to pack sunscreen.

Just as she had begun to relax and ease the aches of long-distance travel from her weary limbs, she heard Nick on the phone.

"What the hell?"

She turned and looked at her husband. He was pacing up and down the main room, looking agitated.

"What is it?" she asked.

He looked up, frowning at her as if he hadn't been aware she had gone out.

"Uh, it's nothing. Just a message."

She copied his frown. He wouldn't be acting so annoyed if it was nothing, she thought.

"No, really, what is it?" she repeated.

He came out with his own glass of the cool mango juice and sat beside her.

"It's just business stuff."

"Nick, you promised," she said, pouting at him. "You said you wouldn't even think about work while we were away."

"I know, honey. I did promise that. I just wanted to check my messages, that's all. Look, it's nothing that can't wait until we get back."

"It didn't sound like nothing."

"Just drop it, okay? I promised you a nice, relaxing honeymoon and that's what you're going to get."

She was a little taken aback by the way he practically snapped at her but didn't comment, not wanting to agitate him further. It worried her though. She knew from experience just how Nick could get caught up in work, but since they'd got engaged he had made an effort to not let it take over his personal life. Usually when he did it was because there was some important project he was involved in.

"So, Mauritius, huh?" she asked, deciding a change of subject was in order.

"Yup. This is a Club Med resort. A buddy of mine came here on a press junket a few years ago and loved the place. It gets pretty hot here this time of year but when I was looking into places for a honeymoon I thought it would be perfect."

"I'm glad I thought ahead and packed sunscreen," she told him. "I'm going to look like a lobster if this is the kind of weather we're in for."

He leaned over and kissed her nose. "Hmm, I bet you'll be a cute lobster."

She deliberately batted her eyelashes at him. "I bet you say that to all the girls."

"Only to the ones I marry."

"Hmm, how many wives do you plan on having?"

"Only one," he replied, chuckling. "Long as you hold up your end of the deal."

Right, the deal, she thought, her amusement fading. He wanted children. She wasn't even sure she could have children. Still, that was some time in the future.

Chapter Thirteen

"So, what do you want to do for our first evening here?" he asked. "Do you want to have dinner here or go to the restaurant?"

She considered it. Despite the fact they spent most of their evenings at home, she was still a little unsure of how to proceed. Especially when dinner in the villa's private dining room implied an intimacy she wasn't quite ready for.

"Um, why don't we have dinner in one of their restaurants?" she suggested.

He looked disappointed but agreed. Since they were both jet-lagged, they opted for an early dinner. Kate headed in for a shower, making the water temperature cooler than normal hoping it would help her get rid of at least some of her travel weariness.

She changed into a cotton dress. Nick had told her to pack for summer heat but also to have a couple of semi-formal outfits. The dress was casual, with short sleeves and a modest neckline, but not so that it would look odd in a restaurant.

She brushed her hair and tied it back loosely then used a little mascara and eyeliner on her eyes. She added gloss to her lips. The effect was understated but also helped freshen her face somewhat.

Once Nick had showered and changed they left the villa and walked to the restaurant. As with all the eating establishments close to the resort, it had a variety of dishes which catered to an international clientele. Kate glanced at her husband, her lips quirking when she remembered all the times they had gone to their favourite restaurant and she'd dared him to try menu items which were outside of his comfort zone. Maybe he liked to experiment in the kitchen now and then but in his mind, that was better since he knew exactly what went into the dishes. She often teased him about his 'sensitive palate'.

"I know that look," he said.

"What look would that be?" she asked.

"The one that says you're about to tease me for my fussy eating." He crinkled his nose at her. "For your information, missy, I did a lot of research on this place before I came here. Especially the cuisine."

"Oh, you risk taker you," she teased.

He glowered at her, but without heat. "Watch it missy. Someone is looking to get a spanking."

She leaned toward him, conscious of the restaurant patrons on the verandah. "You'd have to catch me first, Sloane."

He let his arm drop down behind her back and squeezed her butt cheek. She gasped, not expecting the move. Especially in such a public setting. When she'd agreed to marry him, she'd made him promise there would be no public displays of affection - nothing so blatant anyway. He still tried to push the envelope.

"That is a PDA and that's a no-no," she told him.

"That is nothing," he replied.

"It's called decorum," she retorted. "Something you still seem to have trouble with. Besides, we're in a foreign country. We don't know how these people take that kind of behaviour."

"Fine, Miss Hospital Corners," he said, grumbling.

"That's Mrs Hospital Corners to you, Mr Sloane, and don't you forget it."

"Has anyone ever told you you can be bossy?"

Well, that was a switch, she thought, considering she'd called him bossy a few times.

"You'd be the first," she replied, chuckling.

"Good evening sir, good evening ma'am," the host, or whatever they called them in Mauritius said as they walked into the restaurant. "Are you here for dinner?" The man had an accent Kate couldn't identify but he spoke English very well.

"Yes, please," Kate told him. "Just the two of us." Nick patted her backside and she aimed a glare at him. "Stop it! Behave yourself."

"I don't think they'd mind," he returned, grabbing her hand and kissing her ring finger before turning to the host. The man was smiling politely. "We're on our honeymoon. We just flew in from New Zealand a couple of hours ago."

"Congratulations sir and ma'am. If you'll come this way, I will show you to one of our best tables."

Kate smiled at him. "Thank you. That's very kind of you." She turned back to her husband but couldn't help laughing at his mischievous expression. She was once again reminded of a kid caught with his hand in the cookie jar. "You are so bad!"

"Aww, you think it's cute," he said. "Admit it."

"I admit nothing," she told him, following the host to the table. He led them outside to the verandah which overlooked the ocean. Tropical plants and trees provided some shade for the area and the light ocean breeze helped keep them cool.

Kate thanked the man as he pulled out the chair for her. The table was in a quiet corner of the verandah, making it fairly intimate.

"May I interest you in some of our specialty drinks?" the man asked, handing them each a menu. "Or perhaps as you are celebrating the occasion of your marriage, some champagne?"

"Champagne would be great. Wouldn't it honey?" Nick said. Kate nodded her agreement.

The host smiled and turned away, leaving them alone at the table. Kate turned to admire the view.

"This is pretty," she said.

"Yeah, I guess," Nick replied.

She snorted at him. "Typical male response."

"Why is it when I say things like that you say it's a typical male thing?"

"Because it is."

"That is such a gross generalisation."

"Okay, let me try this another way. If a woman admires something and calls it pretty, would you think it's just her opinion or would you classify that as a typical female response?"

He grinned at her. "Touché."

They continued to banter back and forth as the champagne was poured into flutes. He grinned at her and raised his glass.

"To us," he said. She lifted her own in reply and they clinked glasses.

Kate found herself relaxing in the peaceful atmosphere of the restaurant as they dined. She supposed it helped that nothing really seemed to have changed between them. They still bantered as they always did, enjoying the mutual teasing. She remembered something she had seen on a video online. It had been an old couple who had been married for over sixty years. They had both emphasised the need for friendship in a marriage.

Nick had pointed out that even in the early twentieth century, the concept of getting married for love was not all that common. Most marriages more than a century ago happened because of some kind of arrangement between families. Kate herself had wondered if love really existed until she'd fallen for her now-husband.

After dinner, they strolled slowly back to their villa. It was only seven local time and the sun was just setting, but her body was still on New Zealand time. While the walk and the food had helped refresh her a little, she began yawning once they entered their room.

"Sorry," she said, covering her mouth. "Guess the jet lag's catching up with me."

Nick nodded. "Yeah, me too."

He suggested she read out on the terrace for a while but Kate could barely manage a chapter before her eyes started closing. She went inside and changed into the singlet top and pyjama pants she usually wore to bed then pulled down the covers. Nick raised an eyebrow at her attire but didn't comment.

She fell asleep within minutes of getting into bed, not even waking when Nick joined her.

She woke several hours later to find him lying on his side, his mouth slightly open. One hand lay almost possessively on her hip. He was snoring but the sound was not irritating as she thought it should be. Kate grinned. It was adorable.

Something must have alerted him as he woke up with a snort. It was just light enough for him to see her face.

"What are you doing?" he asked.

"Watching you."

"Why?"

"You were snoring. It's cute."

"Cute huh? C'mere." He pulled her close and kissed her. Kate closed her eyes as his mouth moved to her neck, just below her earlobe. She moaned softly, the butterflies in her stomach returning with a vengeance. God, was this really happening?

Nick shifted, inserting his leg between hers as he rolled over on top of her. His hand was on her hip, sliding up beneath her singlet top. She could feel the roughness of his leg against the smoothness of her own.

He growled as if in frustration. "You know, there are supposed to be huge benefits to your health by sleeping naked," he said.

She felt herself growing hot. She'd never slept naked in her life. Part of it, she supposed, was the result of what had happened to her parents. Another part of her felt a little shy at sleeping without any clothes on.

"Then again," he continued, "taking clothes off is half the fun of foreplay."

She couldn't help the frisson of desire at the thought of him slowly stripping her, of his hands touching her nude body as it was revealed to him. She moaned again as he kissed her once more in a kiss that gave as much as it took. She was fast learning that as a lover, Nick could be possessive and demanding but just as giving.

He'd barely stripped her top off when his cellphone rang beside the bed. He huffed loudly.

"Who would be calling at this time of the morning?" he grumbled. He rolled over and grabbed the phone, pressing the talk button. "This better be important," he growled.

Kate lay back and watched as he got out of bed and walked across the room, his stride showing his annoyance at being interrupted. He grabbed a robe, cradling the phone with his jaw as he grabbed a robe and put it on over his nakedness, then opened the sliding door.

She didn't hear the conversation but occasionally his voice would rise as he talked. Something was going on that was making him upset, she thought, remembering the message he'd listened to when they'd first arrived.

She rose from the bed, grabbing her top from the end of the bed where Nick had tossed it and put it on, then a bathrobe from the closet. She went outside, watching in concern as he paced back and forth looking more and more agitated. He glanced up at her but continued talking.

He hung up the call five minutes later and walked over to her, giving her a quick hug.

"Sorry," he said.

"What's wrong?"

"It's nothing," he replied, almost dismissively. He kissed her forehead. "Don't worry about it, okay, honey? Why don't you get dressed and sit out here for a bit? The sun will be rising soon and I hear it's spectacular. I can order breakfast for us shortly."

"Nick ..."

"It's fine," he said. "Go on."

She sighed. So much for the honeymoon. Something was going on back home and he clearly didn't want to tell her. They were married. If there was a problem, then shouldn't she know about it?

She did as he suggested and sat watching the sunrise. He was right about it being spectacular. She wished she had a camera so she could have taken a photo of it. Sunrise had always been her favourite part of the day.

Breakfast duly arrived, accompanied by the butler the resort employed for their guests. Unused to that kind of luxury, Kate didn't know how to respond to the man, who went about his job with a smile in response to her quiet thanks.

Nick was quiet at breakfast, spreading cream cheese and some kind of fruit preserve on his croissant. He had a pinched, almost stressed look on his face. Gone was the banter from the evening before.

"Listen," he said. "Why don't you go out and do a bit of sightseeing?"

"What about you?" she asked.

"I've got a conference call on Skype in about an hour."

"Nick, you said no work," she admonished, reminded once again of the promise he had made.

"I know, but it's important. I wouldn't do it if it wasn't."

"You said it was nothing," she told him.

"It's nothing you need to worry about," he said with an edge to his voice. "It's just business stuff, to do with the company. You wouldn't understand it."

She bit her lip, not wanting to start an argument on their first official day of the honeymoon, but it slipped out before she could stop it.

"Are you implying I'm not smart enough to understand?" she asked coolly.

He stared at her. "What?"

"Well, are you?"

"Drop it, Kate!"

She huffed and threw her napkin on the table before standing up. "Fine! I'll leave you to your grouchy mood then."

She went inside and grabbed her bag, ignoring him as he called after her. Part of her still wanted to go back and try to do something to help ease his stress but she was too hurt by the way he had spoken.

The main office of the resort had a number of brochures and she walked over, looking through each one to see if anything suited. The receptionist was very helpful, pointing out various tours she could take. Kate joined a small group and left the resort.

She spent the day on the tour bus, visiting the local tourist spots, but couldn't help thinking of the way they'd left things. Nick was stressed and it hadn't helped when she'd practically bitten his head off. Whatever was going on was something he could very well be trying to protect her from.

Since she'd moved in with him, he'd always made a point of refusing to discuss company business. Well, he'd always been that way really, she thought. She remembered the times he'd told her when work had just about taken over his life and the last thing he wanted was to be forced to choose between his family and his company.

She was tired by the time the tour returned to the resort mid-afternoon. The others in the tour group had been curious about her, wondering why she was on the tour alone, but she hadn't responded to their queries.

She walked back to the villa, her heart jumping when the door opened as she stepped up to the porch. Nick stared at her.

"I was just going to the office to see where you had got to," he said. "You didn't take your phone with you."

"I went on a tour," she told him. "I … I'm sorry. About this morning."

He shook his head. "No, it's me who should be sorry. I shouldn't have snapped at you."

He wrapped his arms around her in a comforting hug and walked with her back inside the villa.

"So a tour huh? Did you enjoy it?" he asked as he poured them both glasses of juice.

She bit her lip. "Yes and no. I mean, it was nice, but I'd much rather have gone with you."

"I know. I'm sorry," he said. "If it's any consolation, I wasn't happy about the phone call this morning."

"Is there anything I can do to help?"

"Thanks, honey, but there isn't anything either of us can do."

"Well, maybe if you told me what was going on …"

"It's better you don't know," he told her, guiding her out to the terrace where they could sit and enjoy the summer sun. "Trust me, I've got my best staff working on the problem."

"So it is to do with the company then?"

He sighed. "Honey, could we please just drop it? I just want to enjoy the time we have here."

The evening passed pleasantly enough but again there was no banter. Nick was obviously still in a bad mood and Kate wasn't going to push things. They stayed up fairly late watching a movie on the pay per view channel and went to bed after midnight. She was confused when her husband just lay on his side, facing away from her.

Chapter Fourteen

His mood wasn't any better when she rose the next morning. He told her at their late breakfast that he again had to take a conference call on Skype. Figuring there wasn't much point in her staying in the villa, she decided to go shopping.

Not seeing anything she liked at the local market, she returned to find Nick had left the villa. He'd left her a note saying he would be back some time after lunch but not to wait for him.

Not feeling particularly hungry, Kate decided to skip lunch. She donned her one-piece swimsuit and covered it up with a white gauze wraparound skirt. She slid her feet into jandals and wandered down to the beach.

There were a few people swimming but since she wasn't a strong swimmer, she chose to just wade in the shallows. The tide pulled at her, unbalancing her a little, but she kept walking along the beach. A few people stared at her as she passed but she ignored them.

"Look out!" a voice suddenly yelled at her.

Kate turned just in time to see a little boy on a body board about to crash into her. She tried to skip out of the way, only to wrench her ankle, landing on her backside in the surf.

"Oh god, I'm so sorry. Are you okay?" a male voice said. It sounded American.

She shaded her eyes against the sun and looked up at the tall man. He was blond with a golden tan, reminding her of one of those California beach boy types she had seen in movies.

"I'm so sorry about that," the man said, holding out a hand to help her up. "My son should have been looking."

"It's probably partly my fault," she replied, grabbing the man's hand. She winced at a sharp jab of pain in her ankle as she put weight on her foot.

The man noticed. "I think you twisted your ankle when you tried to jump out of the way," he said. "I'm Kyle, by the way."

"Kate," she replied.

He helped her limp up the beach so she could sit down on the sand. He gestured toward his son, who looked to be about five or six years old. The boy was dark where his father was fair.

"That's my son, Adam." He waved again at his son. "Adam, come here and apologise to the lady."

The boy ran up. "I'm real sorry miss," he said. "I didn't see you."

"It's all right," she told him.

"Next time, although there better not be a next time, you should check it's clear," Kyle scolded.

"Okay Dad." The boy ran off back to the water.

Kyle shrugged. "Kids. You have any?"

She shook her head. "No. I only just got married."

"So where's your husband then?" He grinned disarmingly. "Doesn't he know it's not a good idea to leave his pretty wife out here all alone?"

"He had business stuff to take care of."

"On your honeymoon? Is the guy nuts? If it were me, I'd say forget the business stuff and I'd never let you leave the bed."

She blushed. "Uh …"

"Sorry. My wife was always telling me I have a big mouth."

"Is your wife …" she began but stopped when she saw the look of grief that flashed across his face.

"My wife died a couple months ago. Cancer," he said. "I promised her I'd take the kid away for a bit after … after everything. It was kind of tough on him." He shrugged. "So right now I'm a beach bum." He peered at her. "Where are you from? I can't place the accent."

"New Zealand," she said. He cocked an eyebrow at her and grinned.

"Yeah? I hear it's real nice there. Not like California."

So she was right when she guessed he was from the States.

She leaned forward, rubbing her throbbing ankle. It didn't appear to be swelling, which was a relief but it still hurt like hell.

"I should get back," she told Kyle. "My husband is probably looking for me."

"He a big guy? Dark blond hair?"

She stared at the American in confusion, wondering how he could possibly know that. "Um, yes. Why?"

"Cause he's coming this way and from the look of him he's about to charge like a bull."

She followed the man's gaze and saw Nick striding toward them. She could see from his expression that he was not happy to see her with another man.

Kyle quickly got up as Nick reached them. Kate stood up, suppressing a gasp of pain as she put her foot down.

"Hi, I'm guessing you're Kate's husband. I was just helping her out after my kid nearly crashed into her."

"I see," Nick replied coolly.

"Yeah, she had a bit of an accident," the blond went on as if oblivious to Nick glaring daggers at him.

"Twisted my ankle," she added. Nick's expression immediately changed to one of concern. He reached for her.

"Katie, are you okay?"

"I'm fine," she said. "It'll probably go away in a few minutes. I was just going to head back."

He nodded and turned back to Kyle. "Tell your son to be more careful," he said.

"Nick, it wasn't his fault. Not completely. I wasn't paying attention."

"You should get that ankle checked out," the Californian advised. "Don't think it's gonna swell, but you can't be too careful."

"Thank you for helping me," she said, taking her husband's proffered arm.

"Hey, no probs," the blond man grinned. "See ya round."

Nick looked down at her. "Are you sure you're okay? Do you need me to carry you?"

"No, I think it'll be okay. I probably just need to rest it for a bit."

It was a slow walk back to the villa. The pain was lessening, assuring her that it was just a slight sprain and nothing too serious. Nick seemed anxious, offering to carry her the rest of the way, which she refused.

He refused to take no for an answer when he suggested she lie down on the bed for a little while. He removed her wet clothes and dumped them on the bathroom floor before helping her into the bedroom. He went back into the bathroom and Kate heard the sound of running water. Nick came back into the bedroom with a facecloth and sat on the bed. He lifted her foot gently and pressed the cloth on the affected area. The cloth was cool and helped relieve the throbbing.

"Does that feel better?" he asked. She nodded, watching as he began gently rubbing her foot.

Kate had never considered a foot to be an erogenous zone but the gentle massage was almost arousing. She looked up at her husband's face, suddenly very aware she was completely naked.

His hand was idly brushing over her skin, lurking almost dangerously close to her breast. She swallowed hard. Even the lightest touch from him made her body tingle with arousal.

He looked at her, his expression unreadable. He leaned forward, pressing his lips lightly to hers. She responded, lifting her hand to his neck, her fingers curling in his hair. His stubble grazed her a little, reminding her of his mood that morning. She could always tell when he was not feeling his best as he didn't bother to shave.

She half-expected there to be some kind of interruption as his kiss deepened, his tongue thrusting forward to meet hers. He continued a slow exploration of her mouth, pressing her against the mattress.

She splayed her hands against his chest, feeling the play of hard muscle beneath the cotton shirt he was wearing. She wanted to explore those muscles without the barrier but wasn't sure how to convey that. Slowly she slid her hands down to pull at the hem of his shirt where it was tucked into his jeans. She touched the bare skin underneath, her hands trembling a little.

Her husband took the hint, pulling his shirt off. Kate shyly began tracing his muscles, feeling them ripple beneath her touch.

"Katie," he said softly.

She looked up into his blue eyes, still a little unsure of herself. She had only been with two men before him and neither experience had been anything spectacular. This was the first time she had felt such intense emotion as she gazed up at the man she had married. What was it about him that was so special, so dear to her?

"Are you sure?" he asked.

She had no idea what he meant by that but it didn't matter. She lifted her head and captured his lips in a tentative kiss, which he returned with a hunger that should have shocked her. Instead, she revelled in it, loving that she could inspire such passion in him.

He pulled away, standing beside the bed to pull off his pants before returning to her. He took her in his arms, kissing her until she was practically breathless. She opened her eyes fully to smile up at him, trying to convey all she felt for him.

His smile was tender as he gazed down at her. She kissed him back, loving the gentleness in his caresses. She closed her eyes as his mouth began exploring her body, her arousal increasing in intensity. She cried out his name as their lovemaking became more passionate; the sensations making her body come alive in ways she had never known before.

Afterward, she lay with his arms around her, his chin resting on her shoulder. She couldn't help thinking about the first time she had slept with someone. She had met him at university and they had been dating for about a month when he took her back to his flat. He'd practically pushed her into going to bed with him, making her feel guilty for wanting to say no. She hadn't intended to have sex with him, preferring to wait until they knew each other better. She'd initially refused until he'd accused her of being a tease.

"What are you thinking about?" Nick asked softly.

She rolled over and looked at her husband. "I'm not sure I should tell you," she said.

He frowned. "Is it that bad?"

"Um, I don't know. Maybe." She bit her lip. "Do you think I'm a tease?"

"What?" His frown deepened.

"Well, do you?"

"Who told you that?"

"There was this guy I knew, back at uni. We dated for about a month." She told him about sleeping with the young man. Nick held her close.

"Honey, no. First of all, you are not a tease for telling him no. He should have respected that. The fact that he didn't … that was rape. It shouldn't have mattered that you'd been dating for a month. Hell, a month isn't nearly long enough. Especially when it's your first time."

She had never thought about it being rape before, despite having read a number of articles about the subject.

"I'm so sorry you went through that," he said, caressing her gently. "No woman should ever have to experience that."

"Have you, I mean, did you …" She wasn't sure what she was asking him but it didn't matter. He seemed to understand anyway. That was one thing she had always loved about their relationship. He had a way of knowing what she was trying to say.

He looked at her sombrely. "Don't get me wrong. I've not exactly been a pillar of virtue."

Kate couldn't help the giggle that escaped at the odd phrase.

"Pillar of virtue?" she chortled. He jabbed her in the ribs, making her laugh harder. "Oh my god, I can't believe you said that," she continued.

"Laugh now, missy," he said, rolling on top of her.

She tried to jab him back in the ribs but he grabbed her wrists, pushing her arms up above her head. She squealed as he tickled her, wriggling in the bed. They wrestled playfully, their laughter echoing in the bedroom.

Another round of lovemaking ensued and the room filled with their cries of passion. Desire sated, she lay with her head on his chest. Still curious about what he'd been going to tell her, she leaned on one elbow and looked down at him.

"So are you going to tell me?

He looked at her with sleepy eyes. "Tell you what?"

"About how you were no 'pillar of virtue'," she replied with a mischievous grin.

He poked her. "You are trouble, Mrs Sloane."

"Isn't that why you married me?"

"Hmm, no, I married you because you're gorgeous and we're going to have the cutest kids in the world."

There it was again, the little reminder of their deal. Kate shook the thought away, not wanting it to cloud the moment. Nick brushed the long hair away from her face.

"I slept with a few women in my twenties. And yes, I did have a few one-night stands. I'm not proud of that, but I can't apologise for it either."

"I don't expect you to," she told him. "That was before we even knew each other."

"When I made those promises to you about honouring our vows, I meant it. I don't believe in infidelity in a marriage. When I married you, it was for keeps."

"I know," she said, wishing it was really as simple as that. Nick was an honourable man, she had no doubt about that. She still couldn't help but wonder what would happen if he fell in love with someone else.

"My dad cheated on Mum," he said. "She doesn't think I know about it, but I found out a few years ago. I was just a baby. She was tired all the time from taking care of me and he didn't like it. He never wanted to be a father."

"I'm sorry," she said.

"I worry sometimes," he continued. "That I might be just as bad a father as he was."

She shook her head. "The fact that you worry tells me that you'll be a great father," she told him. He frowned at her.

"But how do you know?"

"Because you wouldn't worry if you didn't care. Your dad … maybe he just didn't care enough about you and your mum. And it's his loss because your mum is an amazing woman. I love her to bits."

"Yeah, she feels the same way about you. When I told her I wanted to marry you she told me I would never find anyone better. That you were perfect."

She snickered. "Oh, I doubt that."

He kissed her. "Babe, don't get me wrong. You can be a bear sometimes, especially when it's that time of the month. And yeah, you can get a little down on yourself, but that's when I can be there to pick you up and tell you you're being a grouch."

"Gee thanks. Just what a girl wants to hear."

"Well, it goes both ways you know. I mean, I'm hardly a morning person and I am horrible before I've had my first coffee."

"Yeah, don't I know it."

He poked her again. "You didn't have to agree with me," he said, sticking out his lower lip.

She suppressed a giggle. "Oh no, not the Sloane pout!"

He rolled them over in the bed until he was on top of her.

"You're gonna get it now!" he pretended to growl. Kate was soon squealing and begging for mercy.

Chapter Fifteen

She couldn't believe their holiday was at an end. Kate sighed as she folded her clothes and packed them in her suitcase. Her husband's arms wrapped around her waist and squeezed.

"I wish we didn't have to go back," she said.

"I know, but sadly we do have to return to reality."

The past week or so had been almost idyllic. When they hadn't been making love, they'd been out exploring everything Mauritius had to offer. Nick had booked them on a one-day cruise to go dolphin watching and he'd also paid for a private session with a photographer. They would have plenty of shots to take home. Not that she needed them for the memories.

The best moment for her had been when they'd decided to explore the local shopping district on what passed for scooters. Nick was good at a lot of things but he didn't seem to be able to get the hang of the small mopeds, falling off several times. Kate had dissolved into fits of giggles which had earned her a look of reproach from her husband. When they'd finally made it back to the villa he'd chased her down to the beach, pretending to wrestle with her in the water.

They'd met up with Kyle and his son a couple of times and Nick had enjoyed getting to know the Californian. The two men had begun a mock argument on the merits of rugby versus grid-iron which had both Kate and Adam rolling their eyes.

Kyle had left for home a couple of days earlier, but not before exchanging email addresses and promising he would visit New Zealand when he got the chance.

"Come on, honey," Nick said, nudging her. "The shuttle's leaving in about twenty minutes."

She nodded and finished packing, letting him hand the bags to the porter. Once outside she donned sunglasses as she looked back wistfully at the villa. Nick took her hand and smiled at her.

"Maybe we can come back some day," he said. "They have a great deal for families. It would be good to bring our children here."

She looked at him, not wanting to reveal that it bothered her a little that he kept talking about them having children. It wasn't that she didn't want to be a mother, but it just reminded her that that was his reason for getting married in the first place.

"Nick, we only just got married. I think it's going to be a while before kids come along."

"I know," he replied with a shrug. He pulled her close and whispered in her ear. "Of course that doesn't mean we can't get plenty of practice."

She tried to pretend she was scandalised by what he'd said but she couldn't. The truth was, the lovemaking between them far surpassed any dreams she had had of them together. He was an amazing lover: passionate yet totally considerate of her needs.

The flight home felt even longer than the first. Some of it in part was because the plane was full and a mother was sitting behind them with a three-year-old who was obnoxious, to say the least. Every time Kate tried to settle down to doze off the boy would kick her seat and wake her up. Nick tried to get the woman to discipline her child but she only told him off half-heartedly and let him do as he pleased.

Nick grumbled at the woman's attitude, telling his wife that when they did have kids, God forbid he ever let them act that obnoxious.

They were both grouchy and over-tired when they finally got home at around midnight local time. Security problems at Auckland International Airport had caused them to miss their connecting flight. Nick had to shell out another hundred dollars each just to get on the next available flight, which didn't fly direct. Instead, it flew into Wellington airport, an hour's flight away from Auckland and they had to wait another hour in Wellington for the flight home.

Consequently, they were both so tired they fell into bed, barely saying a word to each other.

It felt like she had barely fallen asleep when Kate was woken by the shrill ring of the telephone. She burrowed under the blanket, despite the heat already in the bedroom and tried to ignore it. After a few rings, Nick answered it, his voice sounding more than a little husky.

"Sloane. What? We only just got … All right, all right. Give me some time to wake up and make myself look at least half presentable. Right. I'll see you in an hour or so."

She rolled over and opened her eyes. Nick was sitting on the side of the bed, his head in his hands. She reached out, putting a hand on his shoulder, but he abruptly pulled away.

"Nick?" she asked, confused.

"Sorry. Migraine," he said. "I have to go into work."

"But we just got home," she protested.

"I know!" he snapped. "Do you think I like it? Goddamn stupid ..." She didn't hear the rest as he disappeared into the bathroom. She heard the water running in the shower.

Great, she thought. Back to reality with a vengeance.

She glanced at the clock and saw it was a little past eight-thirty. While she was still tired from the long flight, she figured she might as well get up and make sure Nick at least had something to wake him up.

She grabbed her yoga pants from the drawer and put them on, donning a long t-shirt, then went downstairs to the kitchen. She filled the coffee pot and put it on to heat then rummaged through the pantry. They had been planning on going shopping for groceries together on their return but it looked like she would have to go by herself. There wasn't much in the way of food except for a couple of protein bars which Nick often ate when he was on a health kick.

It was better than nothing.

Her husband looked pale when he came downstairs, dressed for work in black pants and a shirt and tie. His hair was wet, the ends still dripping as if he hadn't bothered to dry it. He looked to be in a lot of pain, grabbing the bottle of medication and swallowing the pill dry.

Kate shook her head disapprovingly but said nothing, handing him a cup of black coffee. He took one of the protein bars.

"We were supposed to go grocery shopping when we got back," she said apologetically.

He shrugged and drank the coffee, a little too fast for her liking.

"You'll burn your tongue," she admonished.

"Don't have time to wait for it to cool down," he responded. He frowned as he looked at the key holder on the wall. "Where are the car keys?"

"We put the keys in the drawer, remember?" she said, opening what she called the junk drawer and taking out a small box where she'd hidden the keys.

"Oh, yeah. Thanks," he returned as he took the car keys. "How are you going to get the shopping home?"

"I'll get a taxi."

He nodded and finished his coffee, moving around the counter to put his cup in the sink.

"We really should think about getting you a car."

"I don't need one right now," she told him.

"Fine. Whatever. Why don't you call Teri or my mum? They'll take you shopping."

"Teri will be at work," she reminded him. "And I'm sure your mum has better things to do."

He shot her a look. He rarely said it but he'd always told her she was too independent for her own good. "Call her anyway. I'm sure she wants to hear all the gossip." He glanced at the clock. "I better go."

She frowned. It was just after nine and he was still barely awake. She wanted to call after him as he walked away, hearing him open the inner door to the garage. It wouldn't do any good, she reasoned. Whatever had him going into the office despite the jet lag was obviously more important than his own needs.

With a resigned shrug, she finished her own coffee and went to shower, feeling much more refreshed by the time she had dried herself off and donned clean clothes. She rang her mother-in-law, who sounded very pleased they were back.

"Hello, darling, did you have a good time?"

"We did," she said. "Mauritius was lovely. It only rained once."

They'd spent the entire rainy day in bed. Kate blushed thinking of the things they'd done in that bed. Diane laughed, sounding happy.

"So what are you doing with yourselves today?" she asked.

"Nick had to go to work."

"What on Earth for?" the older woman asked.

"I don't know. Something blew up when we were away. He had a couple of conference calls about it but he wouldn't tell me anything. He wasn't happy about having to go in to work."

"Well, I'm not surprised," Diane said when Kate told her that her son hadn't been feeling well.

She wondered if the flight back had had anything to do with it. She had made sure to keep hydrated and did manage to doze off once or twice, despite the little brat sitting behind her, but Nick had practically blown his top. She wondered if whatever was going on at work had just added to his stress.

"Anyway," she said. "I have to go grocery shopping. We were going to do it when we got back but I don't think he'll feel like doing anything when he gets home."

"Don't you worry, sweetie. I'll come by and pick you up. We can go for a coffee and you can tell me all about Mauritius. Well, most of it."

"You don't have to ..." she began in protest.

"Now I won't take no for an answer," her mother-in-law replied. "Besides, I have to do my own grocery shopping so it's absolutely no bother."

"All right. Thanks, Mum."

Diane made an odd sound. "You know, that's the first time you've called me Mum."

She didn't know why she had done it, but it seemed so natural. In many ways, Nick's mother had always felt like hers. Once, not long after she and Nick had become engaged, Diane had joked she was going to be the 'monster-in-law'. That was never going to happen, Kate thought. She loved the older woman dearly and had told her so.

She hung up after her mother-in-law told her she would be there in a couple of hours. It left Kate plenty of time to unpack their suitcases and put a load of clothing into the washing machine. While the laundry was being done she decided to do the rest of the housework, singing to herself as she cleaned, dusted and vacuumed.

Nick rang while she was hanging the washing on the line and she ran inside to pick up the phone, a little breathless as she answered it.

"Hello?"

"It's me," he said. "Um, I'm not sure what time I'll be home so don't wait dinner for me."

"Nick ..."

"Sorry. This is going to take all day."

What is? she asked silently, wishing he would just tell her what was going on. It bothered her that he was keeping something from her. What could possibly be so bad or so complicated that he refused to give her any details?

She considered bringing the subject up with Diane when her mother-in-law picked her up but kept quiet on the matter. She didn't want the older woman thinking there were problems already in her marriage. She was probably making a mountain out of a molehill anyway, she decided.

Diane turned up a short while later and drove her to the Full o' Beans café. They often visited the café when her mother-in-law felt like going out for a treat. The staff greeted them cheerily and made their usual.

"How was the honeymoon?" Jing asked Kate.

"It was lovely," she said. "We almost didn't want to come home."

The girl nodded. "I understand."

Diane took her arm and led her to their usual table. The café was fairly full but somehow that table always managed to be empty when they were there.

"So, tell me everything."

"Hmm, it was nice. Really nice. We explored the island a bit. Oh, and we met an American. He was there with his son."

"What about his wife?"

Kate bit her lip. "She died a couple of months earlier. He decided to take his son away for a while so they could have some father-son bonding time."

"He sounds like a good man."

She nodded. "He is. He and Nick got along like a house on fire. Eventually." She told her mother-in-law about her little accident and Nick's initial reaction to Kyle.

The subject finally turned to her husband's work.

"Any idea what this little crisis is?" Diane asked.

"No," she said, shaking her head. "Every time I ask he just completely shuts down."

"Well, maybe he's just trying to protect you, sweetie."

"Maybe. But it's stressing him out enough that he got a migraine this morning. Although maybe part of that was because we got home so late. I swear the flight home was like the flight from hell."

Her mother-in-law sighed in sympathy. "Poor baby," she said. "He always used to get migraines if he didn't get enough sleep. He's probably been worrying himself sick."

"After the first couple of days on the holiday, he was fine."

He'd made a point of not mentioning work, especially after the angry words they'd practically thrown at each other. His job had been a bit of a bone of contention between them. Still, just because he made no mention of his work, it didn't mean he wasn't hiding his worries.

She couldn't help but wonder why he felt the need to protect her at all. She wasn't so fragile that she was going to break if she knew he was having problems with his work.

"The thing about my son is he tends to keep quiet for fear of worrying everyone. He's a lot like his father in that respect. He's never really been all that good at expressing his feelings."

"So what do I do?"

"What you always do. Be there for him. Make sure he gets some rest."

That was easier said than done, she thought. Nick didn't come home until late. She had tried to sit up and wait for him but by ten she couldn't keep her eyes open. She went to bed still not sure whether he was coming home.

Next morning when she woke he was just emerging from the bathroom. She frowned at him.

"What time did you get in?" she asked.

He shrugged. "Eleven, I guess. You were already asleep and I didn't want to wake you."

She glanced at the clock. It was barely after seven. Nick was already dressed in work clothes. He still looked pale, with that washed-out look that indicated he hadn't recovered from yesterday's migraine. She frowned at him.

"You're going in again? This early?"

"I have to," he said.

"You don't have to do anything! You're the boss for Pete's sake!"

He sat on the bed. "I know you don't understand, but …"

"I would if you would just tell me what's going on. Obviously there's some sort of crisis that started while we were away, otherwise you wouldn't be this stressed."

"It's not your concern," he said, frowning at her.

"Not my concern? I'm your wife now. Anything that affects you affects me."

He ran a hand through his hair, tousling it so it looked even more messy than usual. "You don't need to worry about this, all right? It's my problem!"

He was clearly trying to placate her as he'd modified his tone to sound less snappish, but she was still upset at his attitude. Their time away had been wonderful but as soon as they were back home everything had turned to custard.

"Honey, I'm sorry," he said, seeing how upset she was. She had never been able to hide her emotions, which had often been part of the problem when she was working. "I don't mean to snap. But you need to understand that there's nothing you can do." He picked up his jacket. "I really need to get to work."

He leaned over and kissed her quickly. "I'll try to get home by six," he said. "Emphasis on try."

Chapter Sixteen

Two weeks later Kate was beyond annoyed. Nick had been late home every night for the past two weeks, even working weekends. When she did see him his face was grey with exhaustion but he refused to let her take care of him, giving her the brush-off every time.

His attitude hurt. She couldn't understand why he seemed to be so distant. It wasn't as if they'd had a major argument, she thought. Considering they'd barely seen each other in that time, they weren't in each other's sights long enough to even talk, let alone fight.

She was surprised one morning when a courier knocked on the door of the house. She had been filling in application forms for the diploma she had wanted to study, trying to work her way around the web pages. It wasn't that she didn't understand computers. It was that the website's navigation left a lot to be desired.

The ringing of the doorbell was a welcome respite from the half hour or more she'd spent wrestling with the site.

"Mrs Sloane?"

She frowned at the courier driver. She hadn't bought anything and was sure Nick hadn't been expecting anything.

"Yes, that's me," she said.

The man handed her a beautiful bouquet of pink and cream roses. Confused, she signed for them and waited while the man got back into his van and drove off. She closed the door and took the roses into the kitchen, placing them on the counter. A small card fell from the package, landing on the granite top. She picked it up.

I'm sorry I've been neglecting you, it said. Nick, she thought with a heavy sigh. As if flowers could make up for her worries about him.

She began untying the ribbon holding the wrapping in place and a smaller package fell out from between the stems. Kate looked at the small box. It was covered with a velvet fabric and looked expensive. She opened it to find a small diamond pendant.

She huffed loudly. So he was buying her expensive jewellery as well? Did the man know nothing about her?

Kate searched for a vase but couldn't find one, so she decided to use a tall glass jug instead. She filled it with water and placed the roses inside, not bothering to rearrange them or cut the stems. Then she picked up the cordless phone and dialled a number.

Melanie, the company's receptionist, answered on the second ring.

"Sloane Mediacorp. This is Mel. How can I help you?"

"Mel, it's Kate. Can you put me through to Nick?"

There was a pause and a slight edge to Melanie's voice. "Uh, I'm sorry, Kate. He's tied up in meetings and he left word not to be disturbed."

"Even me?"

"I'm sorry. His instructions were …"

"Mel, damn it, I'm his wife. I've barely spoken to him in two weeks! Now put me through!"

She thought the other woman was going to argue with her but instead she put the line on hold. Kate waited impatiently for the line to be picked up by her husband, only to be disappointed when his p.a. Bridget took the call.

"Mrs Sloane, I'm sorry, but he's really busy."

"Bridget, I know you're just doing your job, but I really need to talk to him."

"And his instructions were very specific. No interruptions! From anyone!"

The woman's tone was cool, bordering on hostile. Kate had only met Bridget a few times but each occasion had been memorable by the fact that the other woman, older than her by perhaps a few months, would glare daggers at her. In many ways she was everything Kate wasn't. Blonde, perky - the type of woman men would constantly find reason to flirt with. While Kate knew she was reasonably pretty, she had never had men flock around her the way Bridget always seemed to at office functions.

"Surely you're not including me in ..."

"Like I said, he was very specific."

Kate tried for an assertive tone, even knowing it did no good.

"Bridget, I want to talk to my husband and I want to talk to him now!"

"Well, we don't always get what we want, do we?" the blonde told her, abruptly hanging up the phone.

Kate was suddenly reminded of a television sitcom she'd watched when she was little. One of the younger characters was very fond of using the expression: 'How rude!' That was just the way she felt.

Knowing if she tried calling again Bridget would probably hang up on her, she shrugged it off and went back to what she had been doing before the courier had arrived. She managed to fill in the forms and get them sent off to the university then logged off the computer.

It was a beautiful sunny day and she decided to go for a walk. Of course, long before she had agreed to marry Nick, walking had been a necessity rather than a pleasure. Then when she'd moved in to the house, they had often gone walking together. Her husband had even been talking about getting a dog.

Walking around the lagoon was normally a pleasant stroll but she couldn't help thinking about the past few weeks. The honeymoon on Mauritius had been amazing, in spite of their quarrel the first couple of days. So much that she had had high hopes for their marriage. Once they were back on home soil, however, things had changed drastically. She was sure it wasn't one of those situations where the husband just seemed to become someone else. She knew it had everything to do with Nick's job, but for a man who often talked about never letting work take over his life, that was all it had done for the past few days.

She could be more understanding if only she knew what was really going on, but he still refused to tell her. Diane had tentatively suggested that maybe he thought he was protecting her, which they'd both already considered but she had to wonder what he was supposed to be protecting her from. Surely it couldn't be that bad, she thought.

She saw Nick's car in the driveway when she got home. The front door was open and his briefcase was on the floor. She entered the kitchen and saw him standing with both hands on the counter.

"I see you got the flowers," he said, his tone oddly cool.

"Yes," she replied shortly.

He nodded. "Uh huh. Yeah, that's what I thought."

She rolled her eyes at him. "What have I done now?"

"You were rude to Bridget."

"I was rude? She wouldn't let me talk to you."

"I left specific instructions that I was not to be disturbed!"

"Well, I thought considering I'm your wife, that wouldn't apply to me! If Bridget had spoken to me in a more civil tone instead of being so bloody condescending …"

He ran a hand through his thick blond hair. He had dark circles under his eyes and it seemed to her he had lost weight. He probably hadn't been eating.

"Just what is your problem?" he asked angrily.

She stared at him incredulously. "My problem? My problem is I haven't seen you since we got back. You're always at work yet you won't tell me why. You're even there on weekends!"

"I told you to drop it," he said. "This is none of your business!"

"Fine," she hissed. "If that's the way you feel, then maybe we need to rethink this little deal we have."

He stared at her with a perplexed expression. "What deal? Are you suggesting …" She continued to glare at him, trying to make her meaning very clear. His eyes widened as he realised exactly what she meant. "Hell no, lady. When I said for better for worse and all that, I meant it! There is no way I'm going to let you walk away from this marriage!"

"What marriage?" she spat back at him. "For two people to be involved in a marriage they have to actually be <u>involved</u>, not two ships that pass in the night!"

Kate turned and walked away from him before the urge to burst into tears became too strong. She couldn't even look at him right now.

Not wanting to get into another fight, she left the house once more. She didn't really know where she was going but began walking, too hurt and angry to think rationally. It was still fairly warm but she could feel a slight chill in the air. There was no way she was going to go back in that house for a jacket.

It was hardly surprising that she ended up at her best friend's place about half an hour later. Teri must have seen her walking up the drive as she opened the door and stood in the doorway.

"Nick called me," she said. "I'm guessing you two had a fight."

Kate followed her friend into the house. She had barely opened her mouth before she burst into tears. Teri wrapped her arms around her letting her cry it out. It was a while before she calmed down.

Her friend handed her tissues and let her pull herself together before she asked what happened. Kate told her, breaking off now and then to blow her nose. Teri was quiet for a few moments after she finished.

"Well, it does sound like a pretty bad fight but you were kind of rude to Bridget." Kate stared at her and her friend raised her hands. "Hey, I'm just trying to look at this objectively. I mean, I'm not saying she didn't deserve it, but there might have been a better way to handle it. Anyway, I totally agree with you about her. She's had her eye on Nick from the year dot and doesn't like it that he's completely in love with you."

"No, he's not," she replied. "Teri, the only reason he married me was because he wants kids and to help me out financially."

"Maybe that's what he told you but I see the way he looks at you. The same way you look at him when you think he doesn't see it."

She frowned. Diane had alluded to something similar but she just couldn't see it. Teri patted her hand.

"Why don't I go make us a coffee?" she suggested. "Go freshen up a bit."

Nodding, Kate went to the bathroom and checked her reflection. Her eyes were a little red from crying. She grabbed a facecloth and ran it under warm water, quickly washing her face.

When she came out, she heard Teri on the phone.

"Yes, she's here and she's really upset. No, I'm not just going to tell her to come home. She needs her space right now. Well, maybe if you started listening to her you might actually understand why she's so upset."

Teri looked up and saw her in the doorway. "I said no, Nick. I'm her friend, not yours so of course I'm going to take her side in things. If you want her to come home then you better damn well think about your own attitude."

She hung up the phone, sighing. "Sorry. I wouldn't have talked to him if you didn't want me to."

She shook her head. "It's okay. So he's worried about me?"

"Pretty much." Teri made the coffee and sat down at the table with her. "So I'm guessing this all started when you got back?"

"Yeah. He got a phone call and he's practically been living at the office ever since."

"Has he told you what's been going on?" her friend asked, sipping her coffee.

"No. I've asked him. I mean I'm worried about him. He's been getting headaches a lot lately and I know he's not sleeping well."

The blonde nodded, looking thoughtful. "Yeah, I might have an idea about that. Remember your engagement party? Me and his friend Perry?"

Kate nodded. Teri had chatted with Nick's friend for quite a while. Perry had brought a date but ignored her in favour of Teri.

"Well," Teri continued, "we've sort of been seeing each other. It's mostly been casual but after you and Nick got married it's become sort of serious."

Kate cocked an eyebrow at her. "You and Perry? The man is an incorrigible flirt."

"I know," her friend sighed. "He can be a right pain in the arse and if his ego got any bigger he'd never fit through the door. But he's fun to be with. Anyway, he told me something. Don't ask me how he found out. I mean it's supposed to be confidential and on a need-to-know basis but I think you have a right to know."

Kate frowned at her friend. "What is it?"

"Somebody made a complaint to the Commerce Commission a few weeks ago. Something about a man who was negotiating with Nick about selling his business. Anyway, from what I heard, they tried to say that there was some kind of coercion involved. They've had auditors and an investigator there asking everyone questions."

She stared at her friend in shock. "What?" She remembered the negotiation. Nick had bent over backward to please the owner. They'd gone to dinner with the man once the deal was through and he had seemed fairly happy with the final outcome. He'd even invited them to go fishing on his boat. He was a sweet old man who had spent years running his own small company. It had been his baby but his family hadn't wanted to take it over when he retired. It had been no surprise that he had found it difficult letting go.

"Who would do such a thing?"

"I don't know, but it's got everyone at the office pretty stressed and upset. Almost everyone at the office loves Nick."

Kate didn't fail to notice the 'almost', making her wonder if someone at the office had a grudge against her husband. Who they were and why they had done it was a mystery.

Teri got up to answer the door. She came back in looking a little worried, followed by Nick.

He looked just as upset as Kate had been, his expression contrite. He averted his gaze, looking everywhere but directly at her, even flinching a little when she gazed back at him.

"Katie, I …"

She sighed, having no idea how to handle this. Teri shot Nick a look telling him to back off, but he knelt down by her chair and took her hand.

"Baby, please, I'm sorry. I'm really, really sorry. I acted like an ass and I … I'll do anything to make it up to you."

"Anything?" she said. Teri winked at her. That was a bit of a loaded statement, Kate thought.

"I will crawl on hands and knees if you want me to. I'll fly you to Paris. Rome. Italy."

She snickered. "Rome is in Italy," she told him.

"Okay. I'll fly you to Ireland. You can check out your ancestral home."

"You planning on flying the plane yourself?" she asked.

"I probably could," he replied with a grin.

She sighed and shook her head in exasperation. "You're a hard case, Nick Sloane."

"Does that mean you forgive me?" he asked, putting on what she liked to call the puppy dog expression.

"It means I'll go home with you but we have a bit of talking to do."

Her husband nodded, clearly prepared to agree to anything. She told him to wait for her in the car then hugged her friend.

"Thank you," she said.

"I'm always here if you need me, you know that."

"I know, but it's always nice to show some appreciation."

"Well, you tell that man of yours he better buck his ideas up and treat you nice or I'll have to have some very strong words with him."

Kate grinned at her friend. "You and me both."

She left the house and got in the car. Nick looked at her.

"We could go to dinner," he said. "It's only seven-thirty. I bet the bistro would let us …"

"No," she told him firmly. "If we have to we'll order Chinese takeaways or something but I'm not dressed to go out." She hadn't changed out of the shorts and top she'd worn on her walk and the evening had begun to turn chilly as the sun went down.

Her husband agreed but she could hear the reluctance in his voice. She knew what he was trying to do. He was hoping to avoid the coming discussion by having them eat at a public venue. Kate decided it was high time she put her foot down instead of just going along with everything he wanted.

Chapter Seventeen

They decided on getting takeaways from their favourite shop. It took a few minutes for them to get their order since the shop was fairly popular and a few people had ordered before them. Kate shivered slightly as they waited for their order to come up.

"Are you cold?" Nick asked.

"A little," she said, hugging herself. He took his jacket off and wrapped it around her, not commenting on the reason she had left the house without a jacket.

"Number thirty?" the owner, a man in his late forties called out. He was a lovely man who always greeted them with a cheery smile. He barely knew any English despite having emigrated from China about twenty years earlier. His daughter always helped him out with any communication problems.

Nick stepped up to grab the bag and thanked the man with a smile. He grinned in reply, showing a few teeth missing.

"You have nice night," he said before adding something else in Chinese to his daughter. Kim spoke up.

"My father said he hopes things get better for you and your wife." Kim nodded toward her. "He noticed she looks upset."

Nick bit his lip and glanced at her before turning back to father and daughter.

"Yeah, she was upset for a while but I'm going to make it up to her."

The father said something else in Chinese. Kim smiled at her father, then grinned at them.

"What did he say?" Kate asked.

"It's sort of a proverb. Basically, he's saying that a marriage is only good when husband and wife are kind to each other."

"Sounds like words to live by," Nick replied. "Thanks, Kim."

By the time they'd returned home, the smell of the food had Kate realising she was starving. She had barely eaten all day.

Nick got out plates and dished out the food. They took it into the living room. She had just settled into a comfy chair when he stood up again.

"I should get something to drink," he said.

"It can wait," she replied. "Sit down. Stop avoiding this."

"Katie …"

"Nick, we can't keep going on like this. It's not the way to start a marriage."

"I know. I just …"

"You told me you wanted a real marriage and I meant what I said about a real marriage being a partnership. Which means that whatever we have, whatever troubles we have, we share equally. If that's not what you want, then maybe we need to re-set some boundaries. I'm willing to make this work if you are, but only if you stop keeping things from me. Total honesty, from here on out."

"I can't just ... it's not that ..."

"Nick, what could you possibly be wanting to protect me from by not telling me the truth about what's been going on at work?"

He frowned at her. "You know, don't you?"

"Yes, I know. Teri told me. She heard about it through Perry. They've been seeing each other since November."

He made no comment on the news that their friends were dating but looked pensive.

"I'm sorry. You're right. I was trying to protect you. I mean, I don't have definitive proof, but ..."

"But what? Do you know who made the complaint?"

"I think it might have been Joy."

She stared at him incredulously. "As in my ex-boss Joy? What would she have to gain from this?"

"Maybe try and drive a wedge between us, or punish me for choosing you over her. She was always trying it on with me when you weren't around. She was always gossiping about you behind your back, trying to make you look bad, only it just made her look like a jealous shrew."

"How do you know it's Joy?" she asked.

"Well, like I said, I don't have any proof, but remember the night of our engagement party? She came with a guy from work. He's always had a problem with me. I really don't know what I've done to aggravate him but he was involved in the negotiation with Mr Pearson."

He ran a hand through his hair. "Honey, I'm sorry. For everything. I know you've been worried and you're right. The last two weeks have been pretty stressful. I should have confided in you but I didn't want you to get caught up in this. I mean, if Joy is behind this …"

"That doesn't matter," she said. "Did you think I would go off half-cocked and accuse her?"

He grinned sheepishly. "The thought did occur to me."

She got up from her chair and went to him, holding out her hand so he could pull her down to his lap.

"I've always known Joy could be vindictive. She just never liked it that you chose me over her."

"She always was jealous of you. Let me tell you something, you were far better at running that gallery than she ever will be. She just doesn't have a head for business."

"Well, none of that matters. It's not what I want to do with my life anyway."

"Forgive me?" he asked.

She kissed him gently. "Always," she replied.

She loved him. How could she not forgive him when he really had been thinking of her best interests? She could understand now why he had chosen not to tell her, especially if his suspicions were correct. The last thing she needed was to be exposed to the other woman's vitriol.

She sat on his lap quietly, relaxing in his arms. It was not their first fight and probably wouldn't be their last, but she couldn't walk away from him. In spite of her doubts about his feelings for her, she knew if she left him now it would break her completely. She needed him, more than she had ever needed anyone.

They continued to sit together as they ate their dinner. By the time she put her plate down on the table, she was comfortably full. She turned to him.

"So, how much longer are you going to have to work late?" she asked.

"With any luck, I won't have to. The auditors left today and I'm guessing we'll get a report in a couple of weeks. One of them did tell me they haven't seen anything to be concerned about, but that was on the QT." He sighed heavily. "All I can say is, thank goodness it's over. I've been pretty much a wreck the last few days."

"Yeah," she said. "I know. I know how stressed you've been. That's why I've been so worried."

He hugged her. "You don't have to worry about that anymore. I promise, now that I can get back to working normal hours I'll look after myself better."

She turned her head to look at him. "You don't need to do it alone," she said. "You've got me now. And I think I know the perfect thing to help you de-stress."

He cocked an eyebrow at her. "Oh? What do you have in mind?"

She got up and pulled him up. "Come upstairs with me and I'll show you."

He smirked. "Well, it has been a couple of weeks."

"Not sex!" she told him, rolling her eyes. "You've got sex on the brain."

"Hey, I'm a guy. And I'm married to a gorgeous woman. What do you expect?"

"Flattery will get you nowhere," she replied in a singsong voice.

She led him down the hallway to the guest bathroom. Unlike the ensuite, which was smaller, the bathroom had a large spa bath. Kate sometimes used it when she had had a particularly energetic workout to ease the soreness of her muscles.

"The bathroom?" Nick asked.

"Brilliant observation, Sherlock." She began running water into the bath and added a handful of bath salts to the water, then picked up the bubble bath.

"A bath? And a bubble bath at that. Isn't that kind of girly?"

She snorted at him. "God forbid it should take away your masculinity," she replied, punching him lightly in the shoulder. "It helps relax you. Trust me."

He canted his head, looking dubious. "I don't know. Maybe if you get in there with me."

"That was kind of the idea," she said with a grin. "Now get those clothes off, Sloane."

He smirked at her. "You just wanted your wicked way with me," he returned, stripping off.

"Yeah, that's right. You got me." She leaned over to turn on the jets. "Now get in that bath."

"You first."

She huffed. "You can be a pain in the arse sometimes, Sloane," she said, stripping her own clothes off. He took advantage of her nudity by pressing his own nude body against her. "Stop that. Bath first, then I'll think about other stuff."

"Ooh, goody," he said, slipping into the water and pulling her in with him. She batted at his hands as he stroked her.

"No, no. A bath is for relaxing."

"Oh trust me, baby, this makes me very relaxed."

She shook her head and sighed. "You're incorrigible, Sloane."

"Ahh, you love me."

She shivered as he ran his hands up and down her body with light, feathery strokes. She leaned back against him, closing her eyes in bliss. He captured her lips in a passionate kiss.

"I really am sorry about before," he said softly. "I didn't mean to worry you, or neglect you."

"I know," she said, opening her eyes to look up at him. "I got the message with the flowers. By the way, you're setting the bar very high with roses. I'm going to expect that every time you get caught up in work and neglect your husbandly duties."

"My ... why you little witch!"

She laughed at her husband as he poked her in the ribs. She grabbed his hands before he could find all her ticklish spots, lacing their fingers together. She lay her head against his shoulder, tilting it, demanding another kiss. He obliged, capturing her lips with his, kissing her until they were both panting.

"God, you're amazing, Katie," he said. "I don't know anyone else who will put up with my grouchy moods and everything else."

"What else am I gonna do?" she asked. "Besides, that's what I promised when I married you. Sickness and health, richer or poorer ..."

"For better, for broke," he said. She frowned at him, wondering what he meant by that. Then recalled just how bad her situation had been before she'd agreed to marry him. It was hard for her now to remember those days. She had become so used to the new life.

Still, even if Nick did not earn a six-figure salary, or hadn't been born into a fairly wealthy family, she was sure she would feel the same way about him. He was a good, kind, decent man who had given her the one thing she had never known she needed. A place where she belonged.

"Mmm, you know you're right. This is relaxing," he murmured.

"Told you."

He turned them around so she was now laying with her back against the wall of the bath. She looked up at him, her hands covered in bubbles as she clutched his arms.

"What are you planning?" she asked.

He kissed her. "I think you know," he replied.

She could feel his arousal, see it in his eyes. They hadn't made love since their last night on the island. Yet she felt a little uncertain at the thought of them making love in the bath.

"Nicky," she whispered.

He kissed her again, pulling her close as his hands began to explore her body. She clung to him, her world narrowing itself to focus only on him as they came together.

Suddenly he slipped and his elbow hit the edge of the bath with a dull thud and a splash. "Ow!" he complained. "You know when they write sex scenes in bathtubs in all those books, and all those movies, they never tell you how bloody awkward they can be."

"I could have told you that," she said, unable to stop the giggles. She didn't call him on the fact that he'd just admitted to reading romance books. She figured she could tease him about that later.

"Are you laughing at me, wife?" he asked.

"Who? Me?" she replied, trying to sound innocent. "Never!"

"That does it!" He lifted himself out of the bath, splashing water on the ceramic tile and scooped her up in his arms. She squealed as he walked out of the bathroom, still wet.

"Nick, you'll get the carpet wet!"

He heaved a sigh. "Well, excuse me for trying to have a romantic moment with my wife."

She snorted. "Yeah, and we'll have a wet bed. That's real romantic!"

He set her down and left her standing in the middle of the hallway, then grabbed a fluffy bath sheet and wrapped it around her. She snickered at him. He pretended to bite her nose in retaliation.

"You are trouble, Mrs."

"Takes one to know one," she returned.

He quickly dried her off, then himself before picking her up and carrying her into their bedroom. She kissed him as he set her down, pulling him down on the bed with her.

Chapter Eighteen

Six Months Later

It was a chilly August morning when Kate came back in the house from walking the dog. Nick had got his way and they'd adopted a Labrador cross from the SPCA. The dog was still fairly young and had a bad habit of getting into things if he was left alone for too long. Nick usually took him for early morning walks but he'd had to fly to Auckland the morning before to attend some meetings.

Kate didn't mind walking the dog, even in the cold weather, except for the fact that she'd been feeling a little poorly the past few days. Lately, she had been feeling queasy as soon as she got out of bed. If she ate anything more substantial than dry toast it usually came back up again within an hour.

The dog yapped as she opened the door. The phone was ringing. "Quiet Max," she said. Why the original owner had called him that name she didn't know. She let the dog off his lead and he ran into the living room while she grabbed the cordless handset.

"Hello?"

"Uh, Mrs Sloane? Is your husband at home? I tried the office but ..."

"I'm sorry. He's been away for a couple of days. Meetings in Auckland. He should be back tonight though. Is there something I can do for you?"

"Uh, well, I'm Leonard Schuler. I'm the solicitor looking after the contracts for Belarus Ave."

She frowned. Belarus Ave had been the same street her flat had been on. She had been by there a couple of times in the past few months and had noticed the old house had been torn down. It was now fenced off and a large billboard had been erected advertising a new apartment to be built.

"What about it?" she asked.

"The construction company wanted to go over the contracts for the new apartment block. If you'll please just give him the message and tell him to ring me tomorrow."

"Sure."

She hung up the phone feeling mad as hell. Nick had bought the old house and was planning on turning it into apartments. Why hadn't he told her what he'd done? Had he been manipulating her from the beginning? It was certainly starting to look that way.

"Hellooo?" a voice sang out.

Kate went out to greet her mother-in-law. The dog had got there first and was trying to jump up. Diane fussed over him then sent him back to the living room before turning to Kate with a smile. The two women greeted each other with warm hugs.

"How are you feeling sweetie?"

Considering she'd been throwing up most of the morning and hadn't been able to keep much down, she had been feeling surprisingly upbeat until the phone call. The older woman must have noticed as she frowned.

"Uh-oh. What has my son done now?"

She sighed and shrugged. "You remember that fight we had a few months ago? Not long after we got back from our honeymoon?"

Diane nodded. "Yes, I remember."

"Well, we're about to have another one. And it's going to be a doozy."

"What's happened?"

"I just got a phone call. About an apartment block in Belarus Ave."

Her mother-in-law frowned. "Where your flat was?"

Kate nodded. "Yes." She quickly told her about the phone call. "Did you know he bought the house?"

Diane's cheeks reddened. "Well, I knew he'd bought a property. I didn't know it was that. I'm sorry, sweetie."

She sighed. "It's just that … after everything I said about total honesty, he goes and keeps something like this from me."

"Well, maybe he was worried about how you'd react if you knew."

"Am I wrong to be angry? It feels like this whole thing has just been him manipulating me from the start."

"Darling, I know you're upset, but … look, you know I love you, but there are some things I've been wanting to say for a while. Let me ask you this. Do you really think Nick would do something like this to play games with you?"

"He was trying to get me to marry him," Kate pointed out. "I'd lost my job and I was about to lose my home. It was practically the last straw."

"Well, yes, I can see how that would make you upset, sweetie, but when it comes to his feelings for you, my son has never really acted rationally."

She frowned. "What does that mean?"

"I mean he's often acted before he's thought about the consequences of his actions. I don't know his reasons for buying the building but I do know that you didn't exactly make things easy for him. You built up so many walls around yourself that he just didn't know how to break them down without resorting to, well, rather unusual tactics, if I do say so myself."

Her frown deepened. She had no idea what her mother-in-law was talking about.

"What walls? I didn't know I had walls."

Diane nodded. "Oh, believe me, you had walls so thick I despaired of him ever getting through to you. He began talking about you a long time before you and I met and I knew you were someone very special to him. Do you know how difficult it is for a mother to have her adult son basically crying on her shoulder wishing there was something she could do to ease his pain?"

"I didn't know …" Kate began. "Has it really been that long?"

"I think since the beginning," her mother-in-law replied. "Nick rang me the day after he met you and told me he'd met someone special. I don't know if he knew then he loved you but there was certainly a spark. But you made it so hard for him to get to know you. He knew there was something not quite right but he didn't know how to broach the subject with you. So I began making some enquiries and I found out about your financial troubles."

Kate stared at her. "I … You …" As much as she adored her mother-in-law, she felt a little uncomfortable knowing it was the older woman who had been prying into her private life.

"Darling, I know I shouldn't have pried but you'll understand when you're a mother. No mother likes to see her child in pain." She patted her arm. "Well, then I met you and I could see that you felt the same for Nick as he did for you but you were so afraid of those feelings. It felt to me that you were punishing yourself for the mistakes of the past and denying yourself the one thing that would have made you happy. Sweetheart, I know you're upset, thinking Nick has manipulated you, but can you really tell me that the past few months have been so unhappy?"

She shook her head. The truth was, she was happier than she could ever remember being. She was so in love with her husband that she could forgive him anything. Even the thought that he might not return those feelings didn't change that.

She looked at her mother-in-law, eyes wide, finally absorbing everything the older woman had told her.

"So, he does love me," she said.

Diane looked at her with almost an incredulous expression, as if she could not believe Kate was still so unaware of her husband's feelings.

"Of course he does. Don't you remember me telling you he's always had trouble expressing his feelings?"

She nodded. That was true. Maybe he'd never actually said the words but she realised that everything he did showed his love for her. From the way he'd persisted with his proposal to going out of his way to please her, taking her shopping, even the times when he would just hold her hand while they walked together.

"God," she groaned. "I'm such an idiot!"

"No, darling, you're not. You've just let your past blind you. But you can fix that."

She was right, but then Diane usually was. Her mother-in-law grinned at her.

"How about I make us some coffee?" she suggested. "I want to hear all about your studies."

Kate grimaced. "Ugh, no coffee for me. I don't know what it is but lately, the smell of coffee just nauseates me."

The older woman frowned at her, looking concerned. "You did say you weren't feeling that great this morning."

"I'm okay now," she assured her. "I was just throwing up when I first got up this morning but I had some dry toast and I've managed to keep that down."

"You know," the other woman mused, "when I was pregnant with Nick I threw up almost everything I ate." She looked at her thoughtfully. "When did you have your last …"

She thought for a moment. "Uh, actually, I can't remember the exact date but, hmm, let's see …" She'd gone out with Nick for a business function but hadn't been feeling up to par. Her stomach had been hurting, as it normally did when she got her 'monthly'. That had been at least six weeks ago, she decided.

"You should make an appointment with your GP," Diane suggested.

She nodded. "Yeah, I'll do that." But first, she thought, she had to deal with her idiot husband.

Late that afternoon, she drove to the airport in Nick's car to pick him up. They still hadn't got around to getting her a car of her own but she wasn't particularly worried. Although, she thought, if she was pregnant they would have to do something about that. Walking with a baby and carrying every necessity, like a nappy bag and bottles, was no easy task.

She had decided not to say anything to her husband about the property, or the possibility she was pregnant until they were safely at home. He would probably worry that she would be angry with him. While she had been mad at first, the talk with her mother-in-law had opened her eyes.

He looked tired as he left the gate, bag in hand. He'd only been gone two days but those two days had been very full-on with meetings back-to-back. She kissed him in greeting.

"Hi honey," she said. "How was it?"

"Gruelling. I'm glad to be home."

He took her hand as they walked out of the terminal. He shivered as a cold breeze blew from the south-east. The city was situated in a valley and south-easterlies tended to be extremely cold in the winter months. While they didn't get snow in the city itself, sometimes the snow would come down as far as the ranges above the town.

She was quiet as she drove them home. Nick leaned over to kiss her neck and she squirmed.

"Not while I'm driving," she said.

"I missed you."

"You've been gone only two days!"

"Much too long," he told her.

She laughed at him. "You're hopeless!"

He grinned back at her. "But you love me anyway."

"That's debatable!" she shot back, sending him a grin to let him know she was teasing.

He pouted. "You suck!"

"Watch it, mister, or somebody will be sleeping on the couch tonight."

"Yeah? There are two other bedrooms upstairs."

"And what makes you think I'll let you sleep in either of those, Sloane?" she retorted.

"Ooh, now I know I'm in trouble."

"Better believe it, baby!"

She had decided that it would be better for them to talk after Nick had had a chance to relax. He fussed over their dog, playing with him on the floor of the living room while she cooked dinner.

She waited until they were both sitting comfortably on the couch. Dinner was over and the kitchen was clean. Max was stretched out on his own rug in front of the television, lifting his head occasionally to look at them as if hoping they would let him up. Nick had his arm around her and was kissing her neck, obviously hinting for more.

"I had a phone call today. From Mr Schuler. About the construction."

He stopped kissing her neck and lifted his head, his expression showing more than a little guilt.

"Uh ..."

She wanted to tease him, keep him hanging for a little while and make him think she was mad at him, but she was through playing games.

"Why didn't you tell me you bought that old house from my landlord?" she asked, turning to face him. He fidgeted.

"I, uh, I was going to say something but then when you said you'd marry me, I figured it was best to let it lie. I didn't want you to be mad at me."

"Hmm, now what could possibly make you think I'd be mad at you about that?"

"I thought you might get the wrong idea," he said, averting his gaze.

"You mean, the idea that you'd been manipulating me? Why would I think that?" She kept her tone light but there was no way he could mistake the meaning.

"I know how it sounds, Katie. I just ..."

"Nick, remember that fight we had and I told you then I wanted total honesty? Why didn't you fess up then?"

"Uh ..."

"Am I really that scary?" she asked, fiddling with the buttons on his shirt.

He bit his lip. "Sometimes, yeah. I'm sorry, baby, I should have told you then but you were already upset and I didn't want to make things worse."

She poked him in the ribs. "You're an idiot Nick Sloane. Yes, I was mad at first, but then I had a long talk with your mum. She made me realise that your heart was in the right place, even if the execution left something to be desired."

He shrugged and sighed. "I just couldn't stand to see you so unhappy. I knew you hated that place but you wouldn't look for something else. And, well, I guess maybe it was a little manipulative, but I hoped you'd turn to me. Even if you hadn't agreed to get married, I would have suggested you move in here with me and maybe then I could have got you to fall in love with me."

She snickered. "You really are an idiot you know that? You didn't need to do all that to make me love you because I was already in love with you."

He stared at her, surprised. She went on. "The thing is, I've been just as much of an idiot. Your mum told me a few home truths and I realised she was right. We've both been too busy looking at the bigger picture that we haven't seen what was right in front of us all along." She shook her head. "Is this what our kid is going to have to look forward to? Two idiot parents who can't get their heads out of their asses ..."

She was forced to break off when her husband pulled her into his arms and laid the most amazing, passionate kiss on her. She was left dazed and breathless when they broke apart.

He gazed at her for a long moment, his eyes expressing the love he could never verbalise. She smiled softly at him, wondering how she could have ever thought this man didn't love her. Even if he had never said it, he still expressed it in the way he touched her.

She made no comment as he got up from the couch, taking her hand and leading her upstairs. She kissed him, giving him a loving smile, letting him slowly undress her. They sank down on the bed together, the cries from their lovemaking echoing in the dark bedroom.

Chapter Nineteen

They lay curled together, caressing each other gently, exchanging soft kisses.

"Katie?" Nick asked.

"Mmm?" she said. She stretched, almost like a cat, too comfortable to move.

"You said something about our kid?"

"Caught that huh? I don't know for sure yet. I need to see my GP. But yeah, I've been feeling a bit off - throwing up and stuff."

He kissed her forehead. "First thing tomorrow we'll ring your doctor." She heard the excitement in his voice even if he was trying to downplay it. "I'll come with you."

"All right, honey." She figured it was better to agree but doubted he would be able to go with her if the appointment was during office hours.

The next morning, she woke with the same feeling of nausea that had woken her for most of the past week or so. She pulled away from her husband abruptly. He started awake with a confused sound but she had already scrambled out of bed and run to the bathroom.

She'd always hated throwing up at the best of times and this time was no different. She retched over the toilet, groaning. She started at the hand on her back as Nick began rubbing her soothingly.

"I've got you, honey," he said.

"Ugh," was all she could manage before she retched again. Nick got up and rinsed a facecloth under warm water. He pressed the cloth to her face, gently wiping it.

"You want some water?" he asked.

Water would be so great right now, she thought. She needed something to rinse out the bile.

"I'll be right back," her husband promised. "Stay there."

He was back within a couple of minutes with a glass of water. He helped her to her feet, supporting her with one hand on her back as she stood at the vanity unit and rinsed her mouth out. She brushed her teeth, hating the 'furry' feeling and the bitter taste in her mouth.

"What time does the clinic open?" he asked.

"About eight, I think. We won't get an appointment this early."

"We can still try," he replied. "Come on, let's get you dressed and I'll make you some toast."

She loved the way he took care of her, helping her downstairs and making sure she had some dry toast. He also made her a cup of tea, refusing to let her lift a finger. The nausea finally eased.

"You should go to work," she told her husband.

"No way. I'm taking the day off." He grinned. "I'm the boss so what I say goes."

She cocked an eyebrow at him. "Yeah? Maybe only in the boardroom baby, but not here."

"Is that so? You think I let anyone boss me around?"

"You have to make an exception for me," she told him.

"Why's that?"

"Because I'm the woman you love."

He grinned and kissed her. "Damn straight." He glanced at the clock. "It's eight now. I'm gonna call the clinic."

As luck would have it, they'd had a cancellation and could fit her in at mid-morning. Nick drove her to the clinic and made sure she was comfortable while he paid for the consultation. It was a short wait before the GP called her in. Nick held her hand as she explained her symptoms to the doctor, who agreed it sounded like she was pregnant. He sent her for tests at the lab next door.

They spent the rest of the day shopping at the mall. Nick pulled her into the local baby store, picking up a babies' tee he'd obviously spotted from outside. The t-shirt had an inscription on it: Mummy's Little Angel.

"Cute huh?" he said. "We have to get this."

"Hmm, considering any child of yours is likely to be a little devil, I think no."

"What are you trying to say, wife?"

She grinned at him. "Well, you have to admit, you are trouble."

He pinched her backside. "Takes one to know one."

"Is that so?" she asked, stalking him. He quickly put the t-shirt back on the rack and turned tail. She ran after him, laughing.

The next day was a Saturday. They spent a lazy morning in bed. Kate got up around ten-thirty to make a coffee for Nick and a tea for herself. For once she wasn't feeling nauseated by the aroma of the coffee.

She was deep in thought when Nick came down, wrapping his arms around her waist and kissing her neck.

"Morning gorgeous," he said.

"Mm, good morning darling. What do you want for break … uh, guess that will be brunch now?"

"How about pancakes?" he asked.

Her stomach growled. She loved pancakes with lemon juice and sugar.

"Sounds great."

He turned to start making the batter, picking up the phone when it rang.

"Sloane. Yeah, she's right here." He handed the phone to her. Kate took it with a frown.

"Yes?"

"Mrs Sloane, this is the nurse at the clinic. The doctor wants you to come in and discuss the test results. Are you free at one o'clock?"

"Yes, I'm sure I can make it." She glanced at Nick who was busy making the batter for the pancakes, about to ask him if he wanted to come. Then she remembered he had a board meeting for the gallery that afternoon. She would have to go to the doctor alone.

He looked at her with a frown. "What was that?"

"They want me to see the doctor at one. That's the same time as your board meeting."

He shrugged. "I can miss it." Then he sighed. "Oh wait, no I can't. It's the last meeting."

The art gallery was in deep financial difficulty. While entry was free, it was funded through commissions from the artists who showed their work. Joy's niece had become something of a liability since her aunt had taken her on. From the reports they'd had from both regular customers and the artists, she was lazy and sloppy in her work and unfriendly to any visitors to the gallery.

The decision had been made to close the gallery, which was not going to go down well with Joy. Still, the woman had deserved it. They hadn't been able to prove her involvement in the complaint about Nick's company since the Commission investigator wouldn't give them the identity of the complainant but it all seemed to point to her.

Nick insisted she take the car and drop him off at the gallery before going to her appointment. Kate parked the car outside the building, spotting Joy getting out of her own car. She sent them a sour look as if she was sucking on a lemon. Ignoring the woman's hostility, Kate kissed her husband.

"Love you," she said.

"Love you too," he replied before getting out of the car. Joy must have overheard them as she shot daggers at Kate.

The clinic was usually only open for walk-ins on weekends but it seemed they were making an exception for her. No sooner had Kate given her name to the receptionist when she was whisked away to the doctor's office. He grinned at her.

"Well, I would say congratulations are in order. You're going to have a baby. From my calculations, you're due in early April."

Kate smiled back at him. Nick was going to be so happy, she thought. She could barely contain her own happiness. She listened as the doctor gave her instructions and printed out a prescription for pre-natal vitamins and made an appointment for a check-up in another month's time. He also sent off a referral to the hospital for an ultrasound but told her all her tests showed she was healthy and strong and he didn't foresee any problems for her pregnancy.

Still giddy with the news, Kate drove back to the gallery and sat outside the boardroom doors waiting for the meeting to finish. She began reading a novel on her

Kindle, becoming so deeply absorbed in the story she didn't realise the meeting had ended until the door was flung open.

Joy glared down at her. "Well! I hope you'll be happy to know the gallery is being closed for good."

Kate stared back at her with a neutral expression. Nick walked out with his mother and grinned when he saw her. He held out his hand and she let him pull her up, kissing him. Joy made a disgusted noise.

"Something on your mind, Joy?" he asked the older woman.

"You two think you've won, don't you?" she said spitefully.

"Well, we have, haven't we?" Kate told her. The woman made an ugly face, pointing a chubby finger at her.

"This is all your fault," she said. "If you hadn't …"

"If I hadn't what? Worked at the gallery? You really think Nick would have been interested in a bitter, twisted witch like you? I mean, that's the real problem, isn't it? He chose me, not you. And that's why you tried to destroy his company."

Joy scowled. "He deserved everything he got."

"And thanks for confirming what we couldn't prove," Nick replied. "You know, the Commission doesn't take kindly to false accusations."

"I don't care. You destroyed my life!"

Kate smirked at her. "Ever hear of the word nepotism?" she asked.

Her former boss stared at her. "What?"

"Nepotism. Favouring a friend or a relative and giving them a job over a much more qualified person. Not that I would ever consider working with you again. Let me put it another way, Joy. You reap what you sow.

You employed your niece and she turned out to be the worst kind of employee. So don't go blaming me for your shortcomings."

"Like you were any better?"

"At least I never ran the gallery into the ground!" Kate returned.

"From all reports, the gallery was actually doing very well when Kate was working for you," Diane told the other woman. "So how about you get off your high horse? You're the one who made a bad business decision, and all because you were jealous of Kate."

"She's only after your money, you know," the woman told Nick bitterly. "She's nothing but a gold-digging little tramp!"

Nick wrapped an arm around her shoulders and glared back at the other woman.

"I warn you now, Joy, if you so much as breathe wrong in the presence of my family, I will make you very sorry," Nick said, his tone making it very clear he meant business. She stared back at him, swallowing hard.

Kate smiled lovingly up at her husband. He lifted her hand and kissed it.

"I love my wife, Joy. And you are nothing but a sad, sad person. Do yourself a favour. Stop blaming everyone else for your mistakes and grow the hell up."

They left the other woman still fuming. Nick gently guided her with a hand at the small of her back as they walked out to the car, his mother following. He sent her a questioning look as she handed over the car keys.

"Yes," she said, knowing exactly what his question was. He broke out in a huge grin. "April," she added, again knowing what he was thinking.

He hugged her, practically whooping for joy. Diane laughed at them.

"I take it you have some good news?" she said.

"Mum, you're going to be a grandma," Nick told her. She made a face.

"Oh no, not Grandma. Nana, maybe." She wrinkled her nose. "We'll discuss it."

Nick decided to take them out for a late lunch at the bistro. He was obviously so excited at the thought of being a father that he wanted to announce it to all and sundry. Kate gently persuaded him to keep quiet for now. At least until the three-month mark.

As they sat down at their table, Diane grinned and waved at someone on the far side.

"There's Perry. With your friend Teresa."

Nick raised his eyebrows. "Huh, and here I thought that wouldn't last. He's always been a bit of a flake."

"Well, maybe Teri's good at keeping him in line," Kate told her husband. Diane excused herself to go to the bathroom.

He snorted. "Yeah, I'm sure that's what it is."

She looked at him with narrowed eyes. "What are you trying to say, Sloane?"

"Um, nothing?" he replied, looking sheepish.

She turned her head to watch her friend. They'd double-dated a few times with the couple and she couldn't help but notice the way the others seemed to bicker as much as she and Nick had done in the beginning of their relationship.

"You know what I think?" she said. "I think they might actually be good for each other. You never know. I bet they'll be married in a year or so."

Nick sent her a sly look. "Why, Mrs Sloane, are you suggesting some kind of wager?"

She fluttered her eyelashes at her husband. "Hmm, what will you give me if I win the bet?"

"How about a romantic holiday, anywhere in the world."

She remembered the night they'd fought and his promise to take her to Paris. And Italy.

"Fine. I bet we'll be attending their wedding in about eighteen months. If I win, Mr Sloane, you have to take me to Europe."

He held out his hand. "I'll take that bet. This is going to be too easy."

She grinned slyly at him, giving him a passionate kiss to seal the deal.

Later that night they lay in bed together. Nick gently caressed her stomach.

"I can't believe there's a baby in there," he said. "Do you think he knows?"

"Knows what, honey? I doubt the baby is aware of anything yet. It's probably only the size of a peanut."

He shrugged. "Yeah, I guess. I just … I can't wait to be a dad."

"I know," she said. She recalled something he'd said long ago. He'd told her he had wanted to get married so he could have a family. That it was part of the deal they'd made. "Nick?"

"Hmm?"

"Do you remember you said something about me sticking to my end of the deal. What did you mean?"

He frowned at her. "When did I say that?" He thought for a moment. "Oh, I remember. On our honeymoon. Did you think I was talking about this?" he said, touching her stomach. "About us having a baby?"

"Well, you did say the reason you wanted to get married was to have a family. I just … I was curious, that's all."

"I meant our vows, babe. For richer, for poorer etcetera, etcetera. 'Til death do us part. That deal."

She kissed him. "Hmm, now that's the kind of deal I like."

"Me too," he replied, rolling her onto her back to seal the deal with a kiss.

Epilogue

Alexander was crying. His mother tried to calm the infant, handing him off to his grandmother as she performed her duties as matron-of-honour to her best friend.

Alexander Nicholas Sloane had come into the world ten months earlier screaming his head off. A sound which thrilled his adoring parents, both exhausted after Kate had been in labour for almost two days.

That sound had been a sign of things to come. Little Alex was a bundle of mischief, trying the patience of not only his parents but the family dog as well. Fortunately, Max the Labrador was made of stern stuff and took the little boy's teasing with good grace.

Kate had wanted to get a babysitter to look after the baby for the day but her best friend wouldn't hear of it. She adored her godson and insisted he be allowed to come to her wedding to Nick's best friend, Perry.

Kate turned to her husband after they'd signed the register.

"You realise you now owe me a holiday in Europe," she told him.

He groaned. "I'm never going to hear the end of this am I?" he said, but he was grinning.

"Nope."

"What else would you like, wife? Would you like me to get down on my knees and announce to everyone here that you were right and I was wrong? Worship at your feet?"

"Well, now there's a start," she returned, laughing at his woeful expression. "I'm teasing darling."

He wrapped his arms around her waist. "Think I don't know that? You wait until I get you home, wife. I'll show you what I think of your teasing."

She grinned back at him. "Ooh, I can't wait."

Nick held out his arms for his son, throwing the giggling infant up in the air. Kate watched her husband and son with a loving gaze as the wedding guests gathered to congratulate the newly married couple. She looked down at the rings on her finger and remembered her own wedding day two years earlier. So much had changed since then. She'd had her doubts about marrying him but it turned out to be the best thing she'd ever done.

Nick held Alex in one arm and reached a hand for her as they began to walk behind the happy couple. She kissed his cheek and he looked at her.

"What was that for?" he asked.

"Just for being you," she replied.

THE END

Phoenix

"Abby was never strong enough to do what needed to be done. She never would have done half the things she's done without me."

Abby was just a small-town reporter with a small-town future until a man imprisoned for a crime he did not commit begged for her help to prove his innocence. When the man is murdered, Abby realises there is much more to the man's story and it leads her down a dangerous and tragic path.

Abby must leave the past behind and become someone else to survive; to stop the man responsible for destroying her world. Like the myth, she rose from the ashes to become Phoenix.

But she may end up paying the ultimate price: her sanity or her life.

Michael Ryan's career as a police officer was all but over; then he was given the opportunity of a lifetime. He chose to turn away from all he knew, giving up on love, until he met her.

Phoenix is determined to seduce Michael in order to infiltrate his world, but her attraction for him begins to get in the way.

They both have a lot of secrets. Will those secrets destroy their love or will they be able to find a way past the lies?

Can Michael save her … from herself?

Second Time Around

"So, Georgia Hayden, how do you plan to convince me to do an interview?"

Georgia Hayden is an established business journalist for a major media company in Auckland, New Zealand. Travelling back from a business conference, she spots an old friend. When Georgia is asked to interview the old friend, he is reluctant.

Business mogul Quinn Masters lost his wife thirteen years ago and left New Zealand for the UK, hoping to raise his daughter away from the attention of the media. When he returns home after twelve years, he knows there will be some speculation but still wants to protect his daughter.

Then Georgia convinces him to do the interview. Neither of them expect to discover a mutual attraction.

They're both gun shy, for their own reasons. If they can just find a way to get past those issues, they may find love is indeed lovelier the second time around.

Sharp Steele

"You seriously want me to work with him? He's a troglodyte!"

All Amanda Steele ever wanted to be was a cop, like her detective father. The trouble is, at nineteen, she's been sheltered by an over-protective parent.

Forced to work as a Girl Friday for a private investigator, Amanda is surprised to get the opportunity of a lifetime. To go undercover at a local high school to investigate a drug problem.

Jim Andersen is a detective, new to the area. When he meets Amanda, his boss' daughter, sparks fly. He considers her to be a spoiled 'princess' and a little too over-confident for her own good.

When Amanda's father asks him to liaise with her on the high school case, Jim just knows he's going to regret it.

Amanda soon learns she has bitten off more than she can chew and gets herself into trouble when a student is murdered. She is forced to turn to Jim, a man she can't stand, for help.